DEATH IN HIGH CIRCLES

ANDREA FRAZER

Death in High Circles

ISBN 9781783759903

This edition published by Accent Press 2015

This book is dedicated to Major Jonathan Redding and Peter Needham, without whom this series could not have been written.

Other Titles by Andrea Frazer

Falconer Files

Death of an Old Git
Choked Off
Inkier than the Sword
Pascal Passion
Murder at the Manse
Music to Die For
Strict and Peculiar
Christmas Mourning
Grave Stones
Death in High Circles
Glasshouse
Bells and Smells

Falconer Files – Brief Cases

Love Me To Death
A Sidecar Named Expire
Battered to Death
Toxic Gossip
Driven To It

All Hallows
Written Out
Death of a Pantomime Cow

Others

Choral Mayhem
The Curious Case of the Black Swan Song

DRAMATIS PERSONAE

Residents of Fallow Fold

Dixon, Lionel – retired solicitor's clerk

Fidgette, Martin and Aggie – retired teachers

Maitland, Melvyn and Marilyn – nomadic tax-ghosts who never settle for long

Ramsbottom, Dale and Sharron – retired salespersons

Wickers, Mabel – widow of a headmaster

Zuckerman, Madison and Duke – retirees from the USA

Chateau, Antoinette – retiree from France

Schmidt, Ferdie and Heidi – early retirees from Germany

Jansen, Joanna and Wieto – retirees from the Netherlands

Officials

Detective Inspector Harry Falconer of the Market Darley CID

Detective Sergeant Davey Carmichael, of the Market Darley CID

Detective Constable Chris Roberts, of the Market Darley CID

Dr Philip Christmas, FME for the Market Darley CID, and resident of Fallow Fold

Dr Honey Dubois, occasional psychiatric consultant to the Market Darley CID

Previously – in the Falconer Files …

Detective Inspector Harry Falconer and Detective Sergeant Davey Carmichael were first paired together when Carmichael was still a uniformed PC, liable to appear with ink stains all over his hands, a purple tongue where he had been sucking his ballpoint pen, and his uniform jacket buttoned awry.

Falconer was the sartorial opposite, being very fastidious about his appearance and his mode of dress. Their attitudes to life were also diametrically opposite, Falconer being emotionally constipated, and Carmichael not only nurturing his inner child, but embodying an outer one as well.

In their first case together, Carmichael met and fell in love with the girl of his dreams, and they subsequently married, after which he adopted her two sons and they recently had a child of their own. They now live in Jasmine Cottage in the village of Castle Farthing, which is, in reality, two cottages knocked into one. They share this home with two dogs, a Chihuahua and a tiny Yorkshire terrier, and the three pups they produced when Carmichael was a little dilatory in taking them to the vet, believing them to be of the same sex.

At the beginning of their partnership, Falconer had one cat, a seal-point Siamese called Mycroft. Since then he has adopted another three cats, named variously Tar Baby, Ruby, and Meep. He is beginning to think he's a soft touch for anything feline that comes his way and needs a home.

Previously in the army for many years, he joined the police force and was eventually posted to Market Darley at his current rank. Carmichael, however, had progressed from Acting DC, to permanent DC, to DS, and is very happy with his lot.

Falconer is unmarried, being extremely backward in coming forward when it comes to affairs of the heart, and has only fallen in love twice: once in their second case together, and again, more recently, with a doctor who liaises with the police force on matters psychological. He lives in Market Darley.

Their personalities are chalk and cheese, and Falconer has spent the best part of their partnership trying to understand some of Carmichael's more bizarre behaviours and fads. Carmichael had spent their time together trying to get the inspector to loosen up a bit and have some fun.

Considering their vastly different outlooks on life, they rub along together quite satisfactorily; each privately thinking the other is a bit weird.

This is their fifteenth chronicled case.

PROLOGUE

The village of Fallow Fold is situated high on the Downs. In early spring, late autumn, and winter it is scoured by winds, but for the time in between these seasonal scourings its position is ideal, with panoramic views of the surrounding countryside, and clean, fresh air, which is a joy to breathe. It is situated about twelve miles south-west of Market Darley.

It is an old village which has retained its ancient buildings, having been discovered early, by both retirees and commuters, who bought the 'olde worlde' picturesque but unliveable wrecks and invested in them heavily. The result is a community so spick and span and well cared for, that it could almost have been designed by Walt Disney himself, to recreate ye olde England ('y' being a letter that, back in the mists of time, use to be pronounced 'th').

Many of its original retirees had now passed on to that great accountant's office in the sky, but their homes have passed on to younger family members, and the original commuters have found ways of living permanently in the village: usually by selling their London properties when a family came along, and it is now a well-inhabited community, with a much better balance of population than before incomers' money first arrived, and rescued it from demolition.

It is, on the face of it, a calm village, where the most disturbing events are squabbles caused by sibling rivalry, which produce the odd outburst on walks through its pretty lanes, and, superficially, seems to be an absolute paradise in which to live and raise a family.

It has also attracted a fair number of international residents, both from those who worked in England and those who had visited it on holiday. They had chosen it for a good place to settle into their dotages, so it has just a whiff of the cosmopolitan about it.

There is now plenty to get involved with in this village, as it boasts a number of hobby circles. The residents have a choice of joining like-minded others in a plethora of activities. There is a knitting and needlecraft circle, a book circle, a gardening circle, groups for growing both flowers (including arranging them) and vegetables, a bridge club, a classical music circle, and the church choir.

Their weekly, fortnightly, or monthly meetings take place in the village hall, one of the two public houses, or the larger properties of individual members. Each of these groups inevitably boasts cross-over members, as one's interests are rarely confined to one subject area. There is also an amateur dramatic group, like all the circles well-attended and enthusiastically enjoyed, but this latter definitely keeping itself to itself – its participants being much too absorbed in learning their lines and actions in the current production to have time to participate in anything else.

Chapter One

Saturday

The two men stood helplessly in A&E, disbelievingly watching the hospital trolley that was being rushed into the emergency admissions bay of Market Darley Hospital.

The shorter man, with mid-brown hair, bowed his head in despair, thinking how easily this dreadful thing could have happened to any of the team, and feeling guilty that he hadn't been able to do more at the scene.

The slightly taller man with the olive complexion was feeling as if he had been hit over the head with an iron bar. He was completely stunned, and simply couldn't believe what had happened, and with such swift, unstoppable inevitability. The man on the trolley was in a bad way, and the faces of those admitting him and in the ambulance had tried to reassure them, but their eyes were grave behind their professionally optimistic expressions.

He stood straight as a ramrod, as if standing to attention, wondering whatever he would do if the man didn't make it. What would happen to his family? Who would replace him in his job? But even more importantly to him, who would replace him not just as a colleague, but as the reliable partner he had become? In his own way, his partner was irreplaceable, and had carved a special place in his heart for the way he conducted both his personal and professional life. Sometimes he had driven him almost to distraction with some of his eccentricities, but he'd never worked with anyone better.

The shorter man grabbed the arm of a doctor who was rushing towards the room into which the trolley had disappeared, and asked if the patient was going to be all right.

'It's not a clear picture yet, but we do need to get him to the operating theatre to stop the internal bleeding. After that, it's all down to how strong his constitution is, and whether there are any complications that we don't know about yet.'

The taller man stood, still staring at the closed doors of the emergency admissions room, tears pouring, unchecked and unnoticed, down his cheeks, his heart breaking for what might have been prevented if either he or his partner had been just that little bit quicker thinking, or had made a move a fraction of a second before that terrible, deadly strike.

For the first time since he had been a child, he prayed silently, not even having indulged sincerely in this occupation during his years in the army. This was one compatriot that he couldn't bear to lose: his life would be so much the poorer for him to continue in any useful pattern, and it was something he knew he would never get over.

Although they rarely showed their respect and affection for each other, it was tacit in their good working relationship, and he couldn't believe that such a pointless attack might deprive him of this unique personality forever.

4

Chapter Two

Friday – Eight Days Previously

Spring had long since arrived, and was wending its lazy way towards summer. The treetops were a lush palette of mixed green salad, and the normally well-trimmed shrubs in gardens were bustling to throw out errant shoots, eager to destroy their manmade symmetry.

The weather was kindly in a way that is never taken for granted in this country; warm days, blue skies with candyfloss clouds and warm gentle zephyrs of breeze followed mild nights, and the countryside, thus cossetted, put on its Sunday best, and dazzled the eyes with its displays of wild flowers and lush verdant pastures, the call of the wood pigeons adding a soporific air to the next best thing to paradise.

It was during the early evening of his day off on such a day as this, that Detective Inspector Harry Falconer was just considering what to prepare for his evening meal, when there was an unexpected ring on the doorbell, followed by a rather urgent knocking on the door itself.

Wondering who on earth this unexpected visitor could be, he went to open it, and answered his own question when he saw a shape through the opaque glass that was as tall as the doorframe. 'Good evening, Carmichael. What can I do for you on this beautiful late spring evening? And why have you got a cat on your shoulder?'

He'd only just noticed this last interesting phenomenon, as he had been contemplating the dread possibility that Carmichael might have all his brood out in his car, just waiting to pay a visit, and thus turn his domestic harmony and tidiness on its head.

'Davey' Carmichael was his DS in the Market Darley CID and, during their first case together he had met a young woman with two children in the village of Castle Farthing, where he now lived. He had courted her, married her, adopted her two sons (as their father was no longer living), and they had since produced a baby daughter who was immediately named Harriet for the inspector – who had, much to his horror, had to deliver the baby.

The Carmichael household also included a pack of tiny dogs and it would appear, at first glance, that this lithe little cat's arrival in their crowded household might have proved the last straw. Falconer set his face in a determined expression and waited for his answer.

'It's Monkey, sir,' Carmichael said, baldly.

'I know which one it is. How could anyone mistake an Abyssinian for any other breed? But what's she doing here with you?' Falconer could not conceive of a situation that would induce Carmichael to take his cat visiting.

'We can't keep her, sir, and I just wondered if ...'

'What's she been up to? I don't want any feline delinquents in my home.'

'Kerry can't cope. She's trying to wean Harriet, but if she leaves the bowl of baby rice for a moment, Monkey's in there like Flynn, and it's all gone by the time Kerry gets back to it. But the main problem is the dogs.'

'The dogs? How can there be a problem with the dogs? She's only a small cat. You coped very well with me there, and that great lump of a dog called Mulligan, all the time we were snowed in at Christmas. What's the problem with such a tiny feline?'

Carmichael had several dogs, all of them in miniature, and at complete odds with the enormous height and build of their owner. His current count was a Chihuahua, a miniature Yorkshire terrier, and their three unexpected offspring, as Carmichael had been too naïve and dilatory to get the original two neutered in good time. There were now three 'Chihua-shire' terriers to add to his menagerie of minute canines, the pups romantically but impractically named by his wife as Little Dream, Fantasy, and Cloud.

'She might be small, but she keeps herding all the dogs, like they were a flock of sheep, and she chases them endlessly. She thinks it's a grand game, but the poor little dogs are terrified – even Mistress Fang and Mr Knuckles.' These were the parent dogs, but still extremely small. 'And I just wondered if you could find it in your heart to give her a home. I don't want to hand her into some anonymous charity organisation, for she's a beautiful cat, and I wouldn't like to lose touch with her completely.'

'Have you had her checked by the vet to see if she's got a chip?'

'Yes, and she hasn't, for some reason, so we've no way of knowing where she ran away from – and returning her to her original owners – which I'd do gladly if only I knew who they were – seems to be impossible. I even put adverts in the local rags, but no one got in touch.'

This was quite a heart-felt plea from Carmichael, who never asked for help unless it was the last resort, and Falconer took pity on the poor young man, replying, 'I'll give her a week's trial, but if it doesn't work out, you'll have to find another solution. That's the best I can offer.'

'Oh, God, thank you so much, sir. I don't know what I'd have done if you hadn't been a cat lover. Kerry will be thrilled that she'll still get news of the little tinker, but Monkey's just too difficult to manage, what with the dogs, the boys, and the new baby. Here she is,' he said, handing her over to his boss, where the cat immediately climbed on to his shoulder and purred loudly in his ear, a strange double purr that he'd never heard before from his other cats, of which he had already accumulated three to add to his original one.

Falconer's current register of feline house-mates was:

Mycroft, who had been an only cat for a long time, and was a seal-point Siamese; Tar Baby, who was a huge black ball of fluff; Ruby, a red-point Siamese, the latter both inherited from an escaped murderer on whom Falconer had developed a tremendous crush, and Meep (pedigree name 'Perfect Cadence'), a silver-spot Bengal he was caring for while its owner, another murderer, was in prison.

'Well, you've got five dogs, two stepsons, although they're adopted now, aren't they, and a new baby to care for. This will leave me with only five cats, so it's got to be easier for me to give her a trial than for you to send her away and never know how she's getting on. Come on, you little tinker, and we'll see what the rest of the gang think of you.'

'Thank you again, sir. I'll be getting back, and tell Kerry and the boys that everything's all right, now that she's living here with Uncle Harry.'

Falconer winced at this mode of address with which the boys had tagged him, 'I did say it was only temporary, Carmichael; remember that.'

'Oh, I know *you*, sir. You're so soft-hearted, you'd never give her up, once you get used to her winning little ways.'

'You mean like herding other animals, and stealing food?'

'Things aren't the same in your house, sir. In ours, they're much more chaotic. I know you'll manage beautifully and, before you know it, she'll just be part of the family.'

As Falconer turned to close the door, very aware of the furry little bundle now nestling on his shoulder, he left Carmichael tripping down the path, mission accomplished, and whistling for sheer joy at this unexpected success.

Entering his living room, one shoulder, of necessity, lower than the other, four furry lumps roused themselves from sleep, their nostrils informing them that there was an interloper in their midst, and they immediately informed their keeper that there was dissent in the ranks.

'Meep, meep-meep-meep!' piped Perfect Cadence.

'Meow-eow!' mewed Tar Baby, in protest.

Both Ruby and Mycroft joined their Siamese voices in their particular and unmistakeable call of, 'Neow-ow-ow! In reply, Monkey gave a little chirrup, and dropped gracefully to the ground, immediately identifying Mycroft as their leader.

She approached him, her belly slung low – what there was of it, for she was a very sleek brown brindled animal. She stopped a little distance from him and chirruped again, then lifted her head and gave a delicate sniff. The other three sat like statues, awaiting developments, Meep making a low growling noise in her throat.

Mycroft sniffed back and tossed his head as he smelt the superficial and unmistakeable fragrance of d-o-g-s, in the plural, then took one long, deep sniff, to investigate further. Then he sat for a moment, as if lost in considering thought, and gave a small yip of acknowledgement, that encouraged the new resident to approach.

Falconer sighed with relief. This was the moment he had been dreading. What if it had turned into a huge cat rumble, with them skidding and thundering all around the house in disapproval at the proposed change in the status quo?

But they hadn't, and if Mycroft gave the paws up to this little feline scrap, then the others would bow to his judgement as head cat.

In Fallow Fold, it being the time of year for planning the activities for the new season, timed to coincide with the academic year, the nominal heads of all the activity circles had their heads bent over calendars, and referred to letters containing dates that certain members couldn't attend. They also had replies to letters requesting that various

9

local or nationally acknowledged experts in their chosen field come to speak at one of their forthcoming meetings, and all these had to be co-ordinated to produce the schedule for the coming season.

There was, of course, much swearing and cursing, as all the information was collated, and certain unpleasant circumstances raised their ugly heads.

Mabel Wickers of Sideways in Ploughman's Lays sighed theatrically in disgust. She could cope with letters of intention to miss certain meetings; what she was finding most frustrating was the in-fighting amongst the readers of the Book Circle about what books should be chosen to read over the next few months.

And, for that matter, who would do readings for those they had already read together, for their day to shine in the village hall, when it was taken over for the best part of two weeks for each circle to publicly demonstrate what they had achieved during the past twelve months. That was a good way ahead, though, and does not come into this story.

Mabel was a short and portly elderly woman with a wicked, dry sense of humour, but this particular problem was an area from which she could derive no fun at all, nor see any bright side. On one side she had a group of readers who insisted that they should all read prize-winning novels, as they obviously had more merit than anything else.

From the complete other end of the spectrum, she had a few members who were vociferous about the sheer joy of 'Aga sagas', and pushed their case in a most unpleasantly pushy manner. Sometimes she felt like giving the whole thing up and just reading what she wanted to, with no interference in her choice, or opinions, of what she had read, from a crowd of silly women who were just squabbling to see who could get the upper hand.

In the end, she simply scribbled down on a piece of

paper, *1066 and All That*, *Five Run Away Together*, and *Babar the Elephant*. Let them see how they like them potatoes! She'd had enough for one day. She could send along the dates of meetings to their collator, Melvyn Maitland, who lived just down the road in a house called Black Beams, and let him do the final timetable.

In fact, she decided to walk down there. At least they offered a good-quality cup of tea in that establishment, which was more than could be said for some other houses she visited on a regular basis, and if there were a biscuit or a slice of cake offered, she could always justify its consumption later by having decided to walk there and back.

At Black Beams, both Melvyn and Marilyn Maitland were at home, and it was Marilyn who opened the door to her, invited her inside and offered coffee and biscuits. Coffee? It wasn't quite what Mabel had expected but, no doubt, the coffee here was as good as the tea, and she accepted gratefully.

'Melvyn's in the study' Marilyn informed her guest.

'He's got a lot of the stuff through for what we call "optional term four". That runs over the summer and is usually badly attended, but it doesn't mean he can skimp on it. So many people want to change times, days, and venues that I reckon he'll end up not only pulling out his hair but chewing off his own beard as well; positively using it like an oral set of worry beads. I'm sure, now that you've arrived, he'll be relieved to take a break and forget all about the whole beastly muddle for half an hour.'

When called for his coffee break, Melvyn appeared out of his study door cursing and swearing in a most venomous way. 'Those bloody Americans!' he yelled, not bothering to moderate his volume because they had a guest: it was only Mabel.

'What about them?' Mabel asked, intrigued to know what they had done to infuriate him so.

'They just don't honour their responsibilities in this village. I mean, Madison runs the Knitting and Needlecraft Circle, and a very good job she usually makes of it, even if her only interest in that whole craft area is quilting. We all know we have a lot of decisions to be made about exhibiting, and the dates for the optional summer term are always difficult, but she's just written me a little note – posted, I might add, not delivered by hand – telling me that their ghastly offspring will be staying with them for three weeks of July, then the whole bang-shoot of them are going back to the US of blasted A for the whole of August.

'That leaves Muggins, not only to work out the dates of the meetings, but also the exhibition. Well, I won't have it. She'll just have to appoint a deputy, and let *her* get on with it. I haven't got time for this! And all I get paid is a tiny percentage from subscriptions and weekly refreshments and membership money.'

Mabel had to admit that it was not much reward for everything that was expected of him. What she didn't know was that both the Maitlands were 'tax ghosts', who never stayed anywhere long enough to register in the cognisance of local bureaucracy, and were beginning to feel that their time in Fallow Fold was nearly at an end.

They had wandered their way around the world during the time they had been a couple, always working on the black, and in small ways. Thus, had they accumulated enough money to keep them on their travels, and made a little bit to put away in the meantime. Their expenses were low, and they were notoriously slow bill-payers.

Mabel made mental notes as Melvyn ranted and raved, took a sip of her coffee, shuddered, took a bite from a biscuit, and shuddered again. The coffee was very cheap instant powder, and the biscuits were soft. That was very unusual. Perhaps they were suffering financially because of the amount of time he had to give up to be archivist and record keeper for all the circles, and didn't have enough time left to do something better paid.

'Put yourself in my position,' she spat, feeling thoroughly out of sorts at the quality of refreshments she had been offered. 'That blasted Book Circle nearly drives me out of my mind with its two warring factions about what sort of books we should list for reading, and I don't get paid a penny. Sometimes I feel like chucking the whole thing up and just reading what I like.'

'Well, why don't you just do it?' replied Melvyn, still out of sorts with his own problems.

'I think I might just do that. And now, if you'll excuse me, I'll leave you to get on with enjoying your sulk.'

She rose, grabbed her handbag, and marched back to the front door. 'Don't leave us in a black mood, Mabel,' pleaded Marilyn.

'I shall leave in any mood I see fit to. No doubt I shall catch up with the both of you when Melvyn's not so peeved.'

When the door had finally closed on their grumpy visitor, Marilyn asked her husband how his schedule was coming along, and he sighed mightily, and said, 'I'll read it to you. I've already had to re-do it once because one of the damned groups planned to change the day of its meeting, but there was such uproar at clashes with other members about other groups they belonged to, that I've had to rearrange it all out again.

'If it's not right this time, they can all go to hell and blue blazes.' Wandering back into his study with Marilyn on his heels, he sat at his desk, lifted a large sheet of cardboard, and intoned, 'Knitting and Needlecraft, Monday afternoons in the village hall – weekly: Monday evening, Bridge at The Retreat – weekly. Tuesday evening, Books at Sideways – fortnightly: that's the only one for that day, thank God.

'Wednesday is Gardening Circle at The Dark House – fortnightly, and Thursday evening, Classical Music in the village hall – fortnightly. Friday's got Flowers in the village hall in the afternoon – monthly and Choir in the evening, weekly in the church. Saturday's the Am Dram meeting, but no one from that group belongs to any of the others because of the amount of time they have to find to learn lines, so thank the Lord for that. At least there won't be any clashes with the members of that circle.

'And that just leaves us with Vegetables in Tally Ho! for Sunday lunchtimes. What a tangled web. I've had enough for today, and I'm now going to have several large drinks to freshen my temper and my patience. I'll get this done on a poster for pinning up in the village hall, then I'm done with it for as long as I can get away with it. I feel like throwing the whole thing back in their faces and telling them to try to sort it out for themselves.'

'But we need the money, Melvyn,' said Marilyn in an anxious voice.

'And don't I know it,' replied Melvyn, and left the room actually growling.

In Rookery Nook, on the Stoney Cross Road, there were also cross words being exchanged about the regular meetings of the circles, and how it affected domestic life for them both. Martin Fidgette was not seeing his wife Aggie's point of view at all.

'I know you want to pursue your interest too, in retirement, but with all these meetings being weekly, fortnightly, or monthly, sometimes they all fall in the same week, and it's just not good enough,' carped Martin, his monotonous voice petulant with self-pity.

'Well, it's hardly my fault if that happens, is it?' snapped back Aggie, glaring at her husband. This week the monthly flower meeting had taken place in the afternoon, which meant that when she got home again on her sturdy bicycle, there was very little time in which to prepare the evening meal before choir practice, which was that same evening. The choir was run by Martin, and he magnanimously permitted them to take their small, elderly car to that particular event, which was a weekly one.

'And,' she continued, 'what about Sundays? You've got to be in the church well before time, to play for the earliest arrivals, then you go straight off to the Tally Ho! for your so-called Vegetable Circle meeting, which is every bloomin' week. I have to cycle myself down there, then heave all the way back home on my own while you're supping beer in the pub, and I just get to come back here and get the dratted roast dinner on for when you deign to return.'

'I really don't see that you couldn't give up one or two or your activities,' Martin replied ungraciously and extremely selfishly. 'A man does need feeding properly, after all.'

'Me? Why should I give up anything?' Counting carefully on her fingers, she declared, with a small sense of victory, 'I go to four clubs, you attend five different activities, and that doesn't include all the time you have to spend in the church just practising the organ. It's you who should give something up, not me.'

'You're my wife, dammit!' He shouted. 'You're supposed to look after me – remember, you promised to obey.'

'So when do I get to retire?' Aggie was getting really angry now.

'When I'm dead and gone, and then you'll still have to look after yourself. I won't have these rushed, shoddy meals! And I won't give up any of my interests. In fact, I'm going to phone old Lionel Dixon now, and join the bloody Bridge Circle as well, and if that means I'm going to be offered a rushed and sub-standard meal on that night as well, because of your damned Knitting Circle, I shall eat at the damned pub instead of here. At least I'll get a good meal there.'

15

'You go over to The Dark House, but don't expect me to have any supper ready for you when you get home. I shall be in bed!' Aggie was really steaming now. 'And you can give my excuses at choir tonight. This unpleasantness has brought on a dreadful case of indigestion, and I think I shall take an early night. Don't forget to lock up before you go to bed.'

And with that, she declined to clear away the plates, and stalked straight upstairs, carrying her latest book up with her. Of course, she'd come down for a cup of tea when Martin had gone, but she wasn't going to tell him that, or about the fruit cake she had bought on her way home from the needlecraft meeting. That would be her little secret until she'd had a goodly wedge or two in private.

Chapter Three

In The Retreat in Ploughman's Lays, Lionel Dixon was already making plans for the next meeting of the Bridge Circle which wasn't until Monday evening. He had purchased new packs of cards for all the tables, with two spare packs, just in case of accidents. People were always misplacing cards, usually high value ones, which he was sure that they carried off in their handbags or pockets had they not had the chance to cheat with them.

His main problem was how to get the members to pay their fair share of what the packs had cost him. There was no point whatsoever in buying cheap playing cards for an enthusiastic group that met weekly; they lasted for practically no time. On this occasion he had bought top quality cards, but knew that they would balk at having to put their hands in their pockets, especially as there was a charge for refreshments, as these came out of Lionel's own pocket, and not courtesy of the WI, which it probably would have done had they used the village hall for their gathering. And much inferior that would have been, too.

He prided himself on his fondant fancies, sausage rolls, jam tarts, and sponge cakes, but the ingredients cost money which he wasn't willing to donate to what, on some occasions, could be a bunch of whingeing ingrates. And he so hated asking for money. A very shy man, he was bold and direct only at the card table. In all other areas of his life he was quiet and retiring, and not very sociable. It seemed to be one of only two aspects of his life where he came alive, these days.

He belonged to no other circles, finding that he had enough company and gossip in one evening to last him for the rest of the week, and had no further desire to seek out others for social intercourse in between these gatherings.

On hearing the telephone's urgent ringing, he cursed quietly and politely under his breath, put down the pack of cards he was checking, and went to answer the shrill voice of interruption.

When he ended the call, however, he was smiling. A new member would be joining them, and that would liven things up considerably, giving him an excuse to mix people up a bit in their fours, and make up another four. He had three odd members at the moment, meaning that three people always had to volunteer to sit out on some of the rubbers. Suddenly he was looking forward to Monday. Something told him it would be a thoroughly enjoyable day.

Two doors away, in Rose Tree Cottage, Ferdie and Heidi Schmidt were also in the midst of a disagreement. They jointly ran the gardening club, with fortnightly meetings on Wednesday afternoons in a back room at the public house, The Dark House, and Ferdie was not happy about the situation.

'It was you who wanted to do this crazy thing. I don't even like gardening. I want to go to the golf club north of Market Darley and play golf. Gardening is a waste of my time in an afternoon.'

'Is golf not the same?' asked Heidi, heatedly. 'You said you wanted us things together to do after we finished working. Here I have arranged for us something, together to do, and you do not want it to do any more. Why are you so selfish being?'

'Me? Selfish? It was you who were signing us up to run that club. You never asked me if I wanted it to do, first. I do not care for gardening. It leaves me hurting after so much work. I do not like talking about it, because it is you who all the garden work here do. I know nothing about the silly little plants. I want to play golf, and that is what I am feeling to do on that day.'

'But I thought you loved the flowers,' said Heidi, sadly.

'I love the flowers you grow and pick and put in the house in a glass vase. Growing them, I do not care for. I don't even know their names. You grow, you tend, you pick. Me, I shall care to play golf on the Friday afternoons now. It is my decision. I have here and now made it. Jawohl!' Neither of them had managed to get the hang of English syntax as yet.

Heidi trailed dejectedly out into her beloved garden and flopped down on a bench, tears in her eyes, so that all the blooms that had arrived with the spring were blurred to her. Why did Ferdie have to be so inflexible? She had spent decades looking after him and now, in early retirement, he could not even spare a couple of hours to spend with her on what, she had sincerely believed, was a shared passion – but this was the first time they had ever had a garden together, as they had lived in an apartment in Germany.

No, Ferdie just spent all his time moving his investments around on the Stock Market, with the Bloomberg channel booming out in the background, and if he wasn't doing that, he was either having a nap, or planning to play golf. Life after work was not the golden experience that she had expected, and she rather wished she had stayed in Germany, where she had left so many girlfriends behind.

Here, she knew hardly anyone, and had hoped that running the Gardening Circle would expose them to new friendships, together. '*Scheisse!*' she cursed, and continued to weep.

Inside Rose Tree Cottage, Ferdie got his golf clubs out from the under-stairs cupboard, and changed into his golfing clothes. He would do as he wished, whenever he wished. Women were inferior, and must learn to respect their betters.

In Lark Cottage in Fold Lane, however, there was nothing but joy and happiness in the air. Antoinette Chateau had spent twenty years working in England and, on taking early retirement, she had returned to France to settle again in her native country. She had found, though, that in her absence, her home country had changed so much, that she was now more English than French, and decided to make her home in a little village she had discovered during her time in her adopted country.

She loved her little cottage and garden, and was an avid member of the Classical Music Circle, the Knitting and Needlecraft Circle, and the Flower Circle. All in all, she couldn't have been more content. She had within the last winter taken in a stray kitten, something she had vowed never to do, and now loved it like the child she had never had. Life was good.

As a non-English incomer, she could have experienced all sorts of resentment and negative behaviour from the other villagers, but she had a vivacious personality, was trim and elegant, and managed not to look at all her age, which was, in fact, seventy-eight. Her appearance, however, suggested she was a good ten to fifteen years younger, and she wafted expensive perfume, which she loved, wherever she walked.

When she wasn't adoring her kitten, Kiki, she listened to opera and sewed, being an expert needlewoman who loved her practical hobby, and had made all the curtains and chair covers for her cottage, and produced something wonderful and unique, rather than mass-produced. Today she sat outside in her back garden observing Kiki watching the birds, and trying her luck at stalking them.

So inept was the little creature that Antoinette had to

laugh out loud at Kiki's face when she missed her target. She was such an entertaining little animal that she couldn't imagine why she had not got herself a cat before. Her delighted tinkling laughter filled the garden, as she took a break from the kitten's activities to survey the booming borders, and felt a small thrill of pride that she had created this little Eden all by herself, for she was not married.

Still in Fallow Fold, other residents were getting on with their Friday evenings in a rather more enjoyable state of mind. Dale and Sharron Ramsbottom, who resided at The White House in Fold Lane, had strolled down the road to their closest pub, The Dark House, and were sitting outside in the balmy evening air, taking an evening drink and discussing their plans for the coming week.

'It's going to be a busy one, and no mistake, Dale,' stated Sharron, pulling at her vodka and tonic with enthusiasm.

'You're not kidding, kidder,' replied her husband in his husky Cockney accent, draining his pint glass. 'You get a handle on how it's going to run, and I'll just get us a refill – fuel for the brain, you know,' and he headed into the bar to carry out this important task. A quick glance over his shoulder produced the query, 'Do you want any crisps or peanuts, while I'm in there?'

'Make it pork scratchings, Dale. I've got a sudden yen for a nice fatty mouthful,' she called after him, and thankfully he didn't reply in his usual ribald way. The Tally Ho! public house served only posh snacks, for which she had no relish. At least here, at The Dark House, you could get good old-fashioned packets of nibbles, with no pretensions to 'foodi-ness'.

She really enjoyed their involvement with growing and gardening. Instead of just selling produce now, they were actually growing it themselves and, even if it did take up a lot of their time, they always had so much to talk about

21

when they had free time together. Early retirement had been a good idea, in her opinion, and the only fly in her ointment was the succession of weekly meetings of the Vegetable Circle in the Tally Ho!

She knew that it was really a lads' social, and that not much talk of vegetable production went on, and yet she was still expected to produce a glorious roast dinner on her husband's return, even though he normally just collapsed into a comfortable armchair and dozed off, after the number of pints he'd consumed. Still, he drank a lot less than when they'd lived and worked in London, and for this she was grateful, and knowing she wasn't the only wife in the village who had this cross to bear.

Also in the pub garden were Joanna and Wieto Jansen, the village's Dutch residents, but they were only concerned with getting a good few glasses of wine down their necks before going home to sample the organic 'weed' they had brought back from Amsterdam on their recent trip back to the Netherlands. They found its use very relaxing, and missed being able to go into a Grasshopper café, or similar establishment, to indulge themselves in this regular treat that they had enjoyed, before moving to po-faced England.

That evening, the telephone rang in Chestnuts in Ploughman's Lays, and Madison Zuckerman trilled, 'It's OK, Duke, honey. I'll get it.' On the other end of the line was Antoinette Chateau, all fired up with an idea she had formulated a little earlier during her time of contemplation in the garden with Kiki, and afterwards waging war against the ever-persistent weeds in her flower beds.

'I 'ad the most marvellous idea,' she informed Madison, 'to form an 'istorical society in the village. It 'as so much 'istory, but the English in'abitants don't seem at all interested in it. I wondered if you and Duke, as fellow non-English residents, would be interested to join me in

this little idea, to see if we can raise any enthusiasm for it.'
Antoinette was incapable of handling aspirates, even
though her English had a better vocabulary than many
native speakers.

'Hey, that's sounds like a great plan. Duke and I won't
be available during July and August, but we could do some
preliminary investigations as to levels of interest, and,
perhaps, give it a go in the autumn. You can count me in.
I'll speak to Duke after we've finished on the phone.'

At the other end of the phone, Antoinette smiled in
innocent happiness. If things went well, she could have her
own little circle to run; something she had wanted to try
since she had first got involved in other hobby groups.
'We could search for 'istories of the buildings in local
newspaper archives, and maybe find information on 'ow
long some of the families 'ave lived here. You like the
idea?'

'I love it!' replied Madison. 'Leave it with me, and I'll
get back to you right after I've spoken to Duke.' Both
women ended the call with a twinkle in their eyes and
smiles on their faces. It was just possible that this could
turn into a battle of wills over who actually ran and
organised this proposed new group.

Back in Market Darley, Falconer had introduced his new
charge to the litter tray, the food bowls, and water bowl,
and now added another dish to the collection of feeding
bowls on his kitchen floor. He at once decided that he
would have to purchase two double bowls to take the place
of the four individual ones he currently had. They took so
much of his kitchen floor space that he was in danger of
running out of places to walk, and he had no intention of
moving out his kitchen table just to accommodate one
more cat.

Someone had said once that a house without a cat was a
home without a heartbeat, and he now had five extras

heartbeats to keep him company. Approaching middle-age as he was, their lively and comforting company was some consolation for the fact that he still had neither a partner nor a family. They filled the hole in his heart he had always reserved for the eventuality of a life partner (wife, preferably, for he was unashamedly old-fashioned) and children, but he was definitely of a mind to think that he had, at last, met the person with whom he wished to spent the rest of his days and sire children.

If only he wasn't so reticent about matters of the heart, and could just churn out romantic sentiments, rather than being the pragmatic and, in the presence of beautiful woman, tongue-tied man that he was.

He decided that it was definitely time to sit down and get to know this Abyssinian furball a little. She didn't seem a mite phased at suddenly moving home and coming into contact with four strange felines, so he flopped into his comfiest armchair and sat her on his chest.

Immediately, she commenced her unusual double purr, and leaned up to lick his face. The regular gang of four slept on, with one eye open, to see what this interloper intended to do. Was she just visiting, or here for good? They'd have to see what they thought of her before making up their minds about whether she would be one of the gang – or, perhaps, the enemy.

After about fifteen minutes of cleaning his five o'clock shadow, Monkey dismounted from his lap and wandered off into the kitchen. She was probably in need of one or more of the cat facilities out there, and he let her go without worry. After all, what trouble could she get into in a kitchen?

He soon found out, as there was a thump followed by a very gentle but unidentifiable hissing sound, which were followed by the exit of the other four cats, in search of what was afoot. No sounds of confrontation or challenge met his ears, and it was another ten minutes before he went out there himself, to put on the kettle for a cup of coffee.

What met his eyes was simply unbelievable. There seemed to have been a blizzard, but at ground level only. Everywhere he looked was white, with the tiniest of blue and pink dots sprinkled in with the dazzling 'snow'. Then, he noticed that the giant-sized packet of washing powder that he always bought, to save having to make unnecessary trips to the shops, was lying on its side, its contents scattered everywhere, with all five of his pets enthusiastically joining in the game, and starting to sneeze from the effects of the soap powder.

It seemed that Monkey had been accepted as a welcome trouble-maker, by the others. It didn't look like he was going to have any say in the matter and, just for a moment, his sympathies went out to Kerry Carmichael, with her five dogs and three children. This extra trouble she just didn't need. With a sigh, he fetched the Dyson, and shooed the cats back into the living room.

After watching a documentary on the television, he switched off the set and noticed that he was completely alone in the room, but he could now hear a bit of cat hooraying upstairs. That needed investigation, although all the doors up there were kept closed. What mischief they could possibly have discovered to get involved with on the landing, he could not imagine.

When he got to the top of the stairs, he stood there, still as stone, horrified to notice that the bathroom door was now standing wide open, and he had another indoor meteorological phenomenon to cope with. He realised that Monkey was a cat clever enough to cope with the concept of door handles, and she had broken into his bathroom for the express purpose of egging the other four to help her shred the jumbo pack of eighteen toilet rolls he had purchased recently.

This had happened before when Meep had first arrived, and he couldn't believe he could have been so naïve as now not to foresee a repeat performance, especially knowing how she had upset the usual running of the Carmichael household, which could cope with a little chaos if anyone's household could.

The white shreds of paper were everywhere. This would require a black sack before he could even consider using the Dyson. Determining to put hooks and eyes on the outside of his upstairs doors, he trudged resignedly downstairs to fetch the big sucky thing, as his pets probably thought of it, and shooed them down ahead of him, where he locked them in the kitchen, until he had things properly cleared up again.

Again, he had already done this once, to deter Meep's exploration, but as she had settled in, they had not been in use, and he had removed them all quite recently when he had had his woodwork repainted. Unusually for him, though, he hadn't put them away tidily, but had completely forgotten what he'd done with them – and didn't have space in his head to spare, thinking about their possible location.

The way he saw it, he could either spend the best part of two or three days looking for the things, or just go to the DIY store and get some more, for who knew what fresh mayhem Monkey could wreak in that elapsed time

In the Carmichael household in Castle Farthing, where things should have been really peaceful after the removal of Monkey's mischievous behaviour, things had taken a turn for the worse. Their neighbour's dog, whom they had doggie-sat during the big snow-in over Christmas, had been booked to stay with them again in the spring.

His owners were celebrating their pearl wedding anniversary this year, and their daughter had booked a week away somewhere warm, not just for celebration, but to compensate, both for the dreadful winter they had just endured and the fact that time had sneaked up on them stealthily.

A knock at the door, just after the children had gone to bed, revealed both the huge dog that was Mulligan, and his owner, on the doorstep, the latter with a big grin on his face. 'Thanks for offering to do this, Davey. You know how much it means to us and to our daughter's family. Here's his leash, his bowls, and his blanket. I'll whizz you down some chow for him in a minute, but then we'll have to get to bed. We have to be up at five thirty for the trip to the airport. You know how inconvenient travel is, now it's so easy to do.'

Chapter Four

Saturday

Falconer's world was no less chaotic when he came downstairs the next morning in his dressing gown to have a cup of coffee before he showered and dressed. Rubbing his eyes – not scratching anywhere, thank God – and running a hand through his hair, he was horrified, when he had a chance to glance around at the downstairs, at the fact that a whirlwind had apparently hit his usually immaculately living quarters while he slept.

His new cat had continued with her opening of doors, and his collection of everyday shoes from the cupboard under the stairs was a scattered mess right across the living room floor, some with their laces chewed and soggy. His wellington boots had been brought out, presumably caught and killed, and were now lying partly consumed by the kitchen door.

The whole feline gang had flopped to their bellies when they heard him coming, and looked up at him now, with expressions of extreme innocence which, if they were human, would have conveyed, 'It wasn't us, honestly. We were just sleeping peacefully when this awful whirlwind came through, and there was nothing we could do about it.'

Temporarily ignoring the mess, Falconer trudged through to the kitchen. The whole thing would have to wait until he'd had a cup of coffee, but how come this hadn't happened in Carmichael's house? He hadn't said a word about the cat being an actual vandal that could conjure up henchmen with a wink of her eye.

Then he remembered. All the doors in Carmichael's house had round handles that had to be turned, not long ones that could just be pulled down. He'd have to do something about that when he had time, but for now, he'd just put some more hooks and eyes on some of the doors of the rooms in which they could wreak the most havoc.

Consequently, he arrived at his desk rather later than his usual hour, and found that Carmichael had not arrived either, and his chair was empty. The third chair, however, was occupied by DC Chris Roberts, recently discharged from hospital, after he had been involved in an unfortunate hit-and-run accident in a nearby village.

This miscreant had his feet up on his desk, a newspaper held out in front of him, and a steaming cup of coffee on his desk. The room also smelled of cigarette smoke, and the young man had evidently been smoking with his head out of the window. Again.

'What have I told you about leaving the building for a cigarette?' Falconer barked, already put out by his ransacked living room earlier.

'Don't do it, guv,' replied Roberts, peering over the top of his newspaper, not even bothering to put it down.

'How many times do I have to tell you before it gets through your thick skull, that you call me "inspector" or "sir". I will not be called guv, and that's final. Now, get that newspaper folded up, get your feet off your desk, and try to see if you can look like you're actually working, for a change. I will not tolerate a work-shy officer who fugs up what is my office too, with filthy cigarette fumes.'

'Sorry, guv ... sir, sorry.' Roberts certainly looked contrite, but the mood would not last for long. He was a truly incorrigible character who was unlikely to reform, in the opinion of other officers at the station. 'You tolerate old John Proudfoot, though, and so does everybody else. He's not so much 'not the sharpest knife in the drawer': he's more of a spoon, and he never seems to do much

30

more than eat, and sleep on the job.'

Falconer gave a deep sigh of defeat, and turned on his heel. Maybe another coffee, in the canteen this time, would improve his temper, for this young DC was doing nothing for his bad mood but exacerbate it.

'I've got a terrible pain in my side,' he heard as he left the office, but he ignored it. He didn't know whether Roberts was turning into a hypochondriac after his two spells in hospital, but he'd certainly had enough time off work since he'd joined them to last a whole career.

As he was sipping his scalding drink, Carmichael entered the canteen looking a real mess. His hair was sticking out in all directions, he was unshaven, he had bags under his eyes, and, when Falconer watched his approach, he noticed that the man had on odd socks.

'Whatever happened to you?' he asked, thinking that his sergeant looked as if he had been dragged through a hedge backwards.

'I thought we'd have a really peaceful evening, with you taking Monkey, but we'd both forgotten that we'd promised to have Mulligan – and he arrived just after we'd got all the kids up to bed last night.

'He wasn't a problem when you stayed with us,' continued Carmichael, as Falconer thought, oh yes he was, but only for me, as I remember it. I had to share my bed with him for the duration. 'Anyway, when he came before, the pups were so tiny that they didn't notice him. This time they were terrified, and we had high-pitched howls until I went downstairs at four this morning and dragged his blanket up to the room he shared with you at Christmas. Then he settled, and the pups finally went to sleep.

'I slept right through the alarm, and so did everyone else, and I didn't wake up until nearly half-past eight. I just got out of bed, rolled into my clothes, and drove here like the clappers. Sorry, sir. I didn't mean to be so late.'

'Did you know you've got odd socks on?'

'At the moment, I feel like I've got odd feet on. I feel like death.'

'Well, I don't, so let's just hope that no one's feeling murderous today,' said Falconer, concluding the conversation while Carmichael collected himself a pint of tea (in the special mug kept for his use only; he was a bit of a favourite with the canteen ladies) and four bacon rolls, just to help the tea settle, as he had missed his breakfast.

After Falconer had sipped another cup of coffee and Carmichael had engulfed his rolls, three doughnuts, and another pint of tea, just to ensure a balanced diet of sweet and savoury, they left the canteen to see if anything had come in by way of telephone for them while they had been absent.

As they passed the front desk, the ever-present Bob Bryant – real name Trevor, but kept very hush-hush – hailed them with the news that there had been a call about vandalism overnight in the out-lying village of Fallow Fold.

'No cause for alarm,' he assured them. 'Probably just teenagers out for a little troublemaking. I've sent PCs Merv Green and Linda Starr out to do a bit of door knocking.'

'What sort of vandalism?' asked the inspector, curious, as vandalism was not something that happened frequently in any of the villages, the small communities usually taking care of any misbehaviour in their midst without bothering the local constabulary.

'Some mildly offensive spray painting on the one of the houses; couple of cars keyed, flower pots thrown around: that sort of stuff, nothing major league. Once the culprits have been identified, their parents will give them hell, and make them pay for the damage themselves, either in actual money, or in chores of restitution. Local justice still has a lot of clout round the villages, where it's easy to identify the miscreant, because there simply isn't a great deal of choice. Not like here in Market Darley, although we don't do so badly ourselves.'

'Did you alert DC Roberts?' asked Falconer. 'He's at a bit of a loose end at the moment.'

'I did, actually, but he said he was much too busy doing something for you. That's why I sent a couple of uniforms.'

'We'll see about that!' the inspector growled back in reply, and headed for the stairs at a fair pace, more than interested in finding out what it was that he had given Roberts to do that was so much more important than the investigation of a new crime, just reported. Carmichael trailed behind him, glad that it was someone else who was out of line, with the boss in this sort of mood. He himself was far too tired to even listen to a lecture, let alone take one in.

At the top of the stairs, Falconer suddenly halted and put his finger to his lips. 'I think we'll see if we can surprise him, so that he doesn't have time to look busy,' he whispered, then crept down to the office door, gathered himself in readiness, and opened it soundlessly.

Roberts was sitting with his chair swivelled so that his back was to the door. He sat there with his mobile phone in one hand, and a chocolate bar in the other, chatting away as if he had all the time in the world – to some friend or other, from the sounds of it. It was only the sound of Carmichael's mighty yawn that attracted his attention at last.

He whirled round, a look of horror on his face, suddenly turned his conversation to a business-like, 'We'll be in touch, sir, if we hear anything,' and tried to look busy. 'Just a lost cat, sir. Nothing to worry about,' he prevaricated, doing his best to look interested in and connected to his work.

'Do you know how long I've been standing here listening to your banal conversation?' Falconer asked, a

33

sardonic smile turning up one corner of his mouth. 'I'm afraid you've been caught red-handed, and I won't stand for this sort of attitude towards police work.

'I know you've had two holidays in the local National Health hospital, and have got used to being waited on, but you're back on duty, now. I've a good mind to see if I can't get you a month or so on traffic. That should wake you up and make you feel grateful to be in plain clothes.'

'Sorry, gu … sir. I don't know what came over me. It must be this awful pain I've got. In my right side, it is, and it just keeps nagging. It won't happen again, I promise.'

'Fortunately, I like pies,' replied Falconer, enigmatically, then continued, 'And Bob Bryant tells me that you were too busy to investigate a report of vandalism out in Fallow Fold. Do you realise that your laziness and lack of enthusiasm has cost the station two – I said *two* – uniformed officers. That won't look good on the budget, will it? "DC Roberts had to catch up on his social life, so time and resources were wasted while an official vehicle and two uniforms were sent instead."

'Pull your finger out and apply yourself. You know full well that Carmichael and I are both rostered to have the afternoon off, and that'll leave you, nominally, in charge. I don't want to come back to the office to a string of complaints about your slack, lacklustre attitude, and I don't want to hear another word about nagging pains in the side. At the moment, you're a nagging pain in the arse to me, and you don't hear me complaining about it. Consider traffic, and think on, lad!'

Falconer sent Carmichael home at eleven thirty, for a chance to sleep off his Mulligan-inspired hangover, and it was not until nearly noon that Green and Starr returned, entering Falconer's office giggling and fooling around.

'Another pair not seriously concentrating on the job,' he muttered grumpily, and asked them what they had discovered in Fallow Fold. Finally settling down, Merv began the debriefing.

'Some old French woman had "Frog" sprayed across her front door, and some of her flower pots smashed. She was in a furious mood, as she's a very keen gardener, and has lived in England for nearly thirty years and doesn't consider herself French any more.'

'There were three cars scratched with sharp objects along their sides,' put in 'Twinkle' Starr, 'And the couple who both run a gardening group had some of the windows in their greenhouse smashed.'

'And some old guy who runs the bridge club complained that he had a death-threat, but he burnt it. I reckon he's round the twist, though; one of those funny, mincing old beggars, who fusses about absolutely everything, but doesn't actually want to get involved.'

'What was the wording of this threat?' asked Falconer, suddenly showing a spark of interest.

'He wouldn't say,' replied Green. 'Said it was personal, and none of our business.'

'I reckon he's making it up to seem important, seeing as how he's such an insignificant little man,' added Starr. 'Anyway, they've organised a meeting in the village hall for tonight, by telephone and grapevine, so that they can try to identify who did the damage, and decide how to stop it happening again.'

At that point, they started to nudge each other and giggle again, and Falconer dismissed them both as no good to him whatsoever, the mood they were in. It must be spring, the sap rising, and love in the air. He could only guess at the reason, the mood he was in.

When he got home, he walked into his living room, took one look around, turned, and walked straight back out again. His first job on this free afternoon would be to go to the DIY store just outside Market Darley, to buy some more hooks and eyes for all his doors, and some of the little gadgets that kept children out of cupboards and drawers.

The fallout he had discovered in the house, he would deal with when he had the means of preventing it happening again. It was useless to clear up and then go out again, as the chaos would just be repeated while he was out.

In Castle Farthing, Carmichael slept the sleep of the just, having collapsed on his bed with his size fifteen boots still on. Mulligan, the cause of his case of exhaustion, dozed outside in the back garden in the spring sunshine, and the pups and their parents happily chased insects, either through the grass, or airborne, now that the giant had been subdued and drugged into sleep by the warmth of the sun.

Harriet slept in her pram, with the sunshade attached, and Kerry sat outside with a cup of tea, enjoying the peace and quiet, as the boys had gone over to their great-aunt Rosemary's for the afternoon, giving their mother half a pound of peace and quiet in which to do absolutely nothing.

All was well in the Carmichael household. For now.

Things were not so rosy in Fallow Fold, where a great deal of anger had been generated by the overnight acts of vandalism.

In the Maitland household, Marilyn woke to find the other side of the bed empty. Melvyn had not managed to get upstairs the night before. She found him downstairs, stinking of bourbon and slumped in an old Windsor chair in the kitchen. With a sigh, she shook his snoring body, and addressed a question to the bleary countenance that finally tried to focus on her.

'Where the hell did you get to, last night? What are you doing skulking down here? Too rat-arsed to get up the stairs, were you?'

Melvyn rubbed his stubbly face and muttered, 'I was

just chilling out with a half of Wild Turkey, when that hyperactive American harpy phoned up, then that disgustingly cheerful French woman, both of them dribbling on about setting up a Historical Circle.'

'And?' Marilyn encouraged him.

'Well, I was so damned sick of all these bloody groups that I just blew my stack, telling them I needed some peace in my life, and that they could go to hell, because I was having a well-earned unwind.'

'Melvyn, you didn't.'

'I did. Or, at least, I think I did. I don't think I dreamt it. After that, I finished the bottle, and moved on to some malt that we had left. I'd had about enough of the whole bunch of them, what with doing this new timetable – change after change, with everyone going off on long holidays at the most inconvenient time.

'Then that awful old biddy came round yesterday afternoon and finally, just when I thought I'd got them all off my back for a while, I had two more phone calls wanting me to do something else for a pittance. I just flipped. Sorry. I'll apologise when I've had a shower, a shave, and a couple of cups of good, strong coffee.'

'You make sure that you do,' his wife retorted. 'The job may not pay much, but we need the money, and you don't declare it anywhere, so we don't have to worry about paying tax. Hmph!'

Before he could prepare himself for his apologies, though, the phone rang yet again, and Melvyn groaned out loud. 'I bet that bloody thing's for me.' And it was. It was an invitation to the village hall that evening to discuss the vandalism that had taken place during the night, and Melvyn received the news of the nocturnal activities with a glum face.

That was his evening gone. He'd have to get round to the shops and stock up on something strong for the latter half of the evening, as he was sure to be in a foul mood again, and need another little relaxer. This time he'd leave the phone off the hook and put in his earphones to listen to a little chill-out music, before he went to bed. It would be nice to actually make it upstairs tonight.

When Falconer got home from the DIY store with his new collection of hooks and eyes and little fiddle-de-dees to stop his new cat from getting to the places where no cat should be, he was prepared to sort through the shredded papers from the top of his desk, as the results of this little attack were what had caught his eye when he returned earlier, and turned on his heel and gone straight out again.

This time, when he entered the house, he was chagrined to find that the local free paper had been delivered in his absence, and was now just a very large pile of slender strips just inside the front door, a few of the tatters having been trailed into the sitting room for playthings. Would he never win? And did he still need an electric paper shredder?

Making a mental note to buy one of those metal mesh mail catchers that could be fitted to the back of front doors, for the sole purpose of preventing this sort of happening, he went to his toolbox for a screwdriver. At least he could keep them out of his other rooms, if he made the effort this evening, and would know that his trip downstairs the following day would not be full of terrible and messy surprises.

He received a tremendous amount of help from the cats in general, on this little DIY mission, as they all tried to catch the screwdriver as he manipulated it, or patted away his next little packet of hooks and eyes, to chase it into some difficult to access corner, and he was sure Barry Bucknell never had this problem in his old black and white television series.

On his bedroom door he fitted two hooks and eyes; one outside to keep the cats out when he wasn't up there, and one inside, to keep them out when he was in bed. That should spike the little games Monkey devised for his undivided, if negative, attention.

Finally, the last fixing was done, and he could retire to the kitchen to see about getting something to eat. He was not a man used to scrabbling about on his knees doing 'little jobs' around the home, and he had raised quite an appetite. He would do something quick and easy.

Or, at least, he would, when he had cleared away the mess that 'Some-cat' had made of the kitchen roll he had left out on the work surface on its holder.

The impromptu meeting in the village hall that night had been scheduled for six thirty, so that the whole evening wasn't taken up with local grumbling, and it was being chaired by Mabel Wickers, a frequent chairperson in her younger years, and an enthusiastic volunteer for such duties in her later ones.

She effortlessly silenced the complaining group of people, and opened the meeting by announcing what had already been reported to her, asking for any further acts of vandalism to be added to her list after the meeting.

'So far, Antoinette Chateau has suffered the unfortunate experience of having the derogatory and inflammatory word "frog" painted on her front door, and some of her beloved pots of plants have been smashed. These were particularly spiteful acts against a harmless and friendly lady who has always participated in the gardening activities of this village with gusto.'

Antoinette relaxed her pained and victimised expression, to give a little smile at such a nice description of her as a good resident.

'The damage to paintwork on cars,' Mabel continued, 'was to the vehicles of Duke Zuckerman, Martin Fidgette, and myself; a cowardly act carried out by a cowardly individual, which will undoubtedly affect our insurance premiums.'

Two male voices from those gathered made fairly loud comments of discontent and anger as this was announced. Martin Fidgette in particular was besotted by his car, to the point that he would not let Aggie drive it at all and, on many occasions when he was not available, she had had to resort to using her bicycle to get where she wanted or needed to be.

'Ferdie and Heidi Schmidt had some of the panes of glass in their greenhouse broken, a consideration that might yet prove catastrophic to their spring seedlings ...'

'I heard something!' shouted Ferdie. 'I definitely heard someone creeping around in the night, but I went back to sleep. I am a very heavy sleeper.'

'You're very heavy, full-stop!' Marilyn Maitland was heard to murmur quietly. Ferdie was not a particularly tall man, but he was broad, and looked a typical German. Many villagers felt intimidated by him, although he was a very friendly and sociable man. Appearances mean so much when someone doesn't know one.

'It is also noted,' continued Mabel, not letting the interruptions make her lose her place in her announcements, 'that Lionel Dixon received a very unpleasant communication, although he doesn't feel able to share its contents with us, because it concerns a personal matter.

'We need to winkle out who did this, and why, for we cannot tolerate such behaviour in our peaceful and happy community. Reports of any further vandalism and, of course, any information that may lead to the apprehension of the perpetrator, to me, please, and I shall co-ordinate and report to the police as necessary.

'Before we finish, I should like to propose that Mr Maitland draws up a rota for a patrol through the village, twice after dark, at unspecified hours. I'll be in touch when he has a timetable worked out. Thank you very much for your time, ladies and gentlemen.'

The meeting officially broke up at that point, leaving twos and threes of people to have private moans with each other and their friends. It had been attended, not just by those affected but, as word had got round, by those who had been left out of the spiteful acts, that they may find out of what to be extra protective, and about what to be on their guard.

Joanna Jansen giggled as she whispered to Wieto, 'I don't suppose it was us that did all that, do you? After all, we were a bit off our faces after that "blow" last night.'

'Don't be stupid,' he replied. 'We'd be aware of any vandalism we'd caused.' And then he added, 'I think!'

Mabel Wickers stumped off home to put what potted plants she had outside into the shed before nightfall. She'd grown everything from seed, and didn't want all her time and care destroyed with a casual kick of an uncaring foot.

Melvyn Maitland was a very unhappy bunny as he stumped back home. Another blasted list to draw up! More people to speak to about when they could help! And would he get an extra penny for this? No, of course he wouldn't! At that moment, he wished he lived anywhere in the world but this picturesque little English village.

Once home, he grabbed the neck of a bottle of rum he had purchased earlier that day, with a glass from the draining board, and headed straight for his study. Seeing the direction in which he was headed, Marilyn called after him, 'Oh, don't go off on another toot tonight, Mel.'

'I shall do what I please in my own blasted home,' he yelled over his shoulder, and slammed shut the door behind him. Was he never to have any peace?

When the German couple got home, Ferdie sat for a while in silence, an expression of dark determination and cunning on his face. 'What do you think about?' asked Heidi, puzzled at what had caused this deep introspection.

41

'I have a little idea,' he announced, looking up at her. 'I will sit up tonight with my little air gun, and if I see any of this mischief-making, I will pot who is doing it, so they can be uncovered and made to pay for their misdeeds.'

'Do you think that wise?' Heidi was sceptical that his plan was a sensible one. 'What if it is you who is arrested?'

'I will be doing my duty as a good citizen, is that not so? You will see! I shall catch the mischief-maker, and hand him over to the police. I shall be a hero in this village. It is true. Believe me. I know this!'

Heidi was troubled at his plan, but knew that any resistance was useless. Once Ferdie had set his mind to do something, it was done, and nothing would distract him from his planned course of action.

The couple made a point of staying up late, watching German TV via satellite. Heidi usually went to bed much earlier than her partner, but tonight she wanted to stay up as late as she could, because she was worried about what he was intending to do.

Eventually, however, when her eyes started to droop, she had to give in and go upstairs. Ferdie immediately began to plan for his night-time vigil, gathering together a few bottles of good German beer, a snack or two to keep up his strength, a fleece in which to wrap himself, for, even though the night was a mild one, being sedentary, he would feel the cold, and Ferdie did not approve of feeling cold.

Finally, he collected a warm hat and his air pistol, and made his way out to their garden shed to set himself up as a human trap. He would leave the shed door open, with no light showing from inside, and from where he had a good view of the garden. If anyone came in search of mischief tonight, he would be well prepared, and mark the miscreant in such a way that he would be easily identifiable by the police.

He would not be bored. He would spend his night thinking about his investment portfolio, and how he might improve his dividends. If he was still not in bed by morning, he could go straight into the house and check the Bloomberg stock market channel, to see if his overnight thoughts might bear fruit.

Heidi went straight to sleep as her head touched the pillow. She was one who never suffered from insomnia, and had no sympathy for others who said they could not get to sleep. It was easy. One just closed one's eyes, turned off the computer in one's head, and sleep descended effortlessly.

Chapter Five

Sunday – The Early Hours

At 2.30 a.m., as Ferdie was right in the middle of planning a complete shake-up in his investment portfolio, his ears caught sounds of movement just beyond the hedge of the back garden. Immediately he put his brain on pause, and channelled all his attention into listening. What he heard was too big to be an animal. He was instantly on the alert. Maybe the maker of mischief was, at this very moment, entering his garden to commit further criminal acts.

Silently, he took up his gun, which had been sitting beside him, and stood up, to take position as an observer, but there was nothing to be seen for now. The crack of a twig brought him to full attention, and he peered cautiously through the open door to see nothing but his own garden bathed in moonlight.

Suddenly, there was a sound dead ahead of him, and he decided it was now time to take action. Leaving the cover of his hideaway, he took one step, then two, outside the shed, only for the moonlit garden to waver and disappear into blackness. His last conscious thought was that whoever it was must have thrown something down the garden to get his attention, but been waiting for him behind the shed's open door.

Heidi woke suddenly at just before three, for no reason that she could explain and, as Ferdie had still not come to bed, decided that she would take him out some coffee with something a little stimulating in it, to warm his bones during his vigil.

She crept down to the kitchen, although she couldn't understand why she did this, as she was the only one in the house, and put the kettle on to make the coffee, then changed her mind. She would not use the horrible instant that they used for emergencies; she would use the state-of-the-art machine that Ferdie had bought her which made a range of different types of coffee. Only the best for her man!

Having filled a thermos flask with the liquid, she added three spoonfuls of sugar and a very large shot of cognac, shook the resulting liquid reviver, then carried it out of the back door to deliver to the shed, still wearing only her dressing gown and slippers.

Oh no! she thought, as she noticed a dark lump just outside the shed. Surely Ferdie had not already hurt someone that badly that they were collapsed? She increased her pace from a walk to a trot, worried about what the police might do to such a person as Ferdie, who always wanted to sort out things his own way.

Setting down the flask delicately, for she was, after all, a practical German, and didn't want to break the delicate interior, Heidi knelt down on the grass to see who Ferdie had shot, while wondering where he was. And suddenly, she knew, for it was he who was unconscious on the ground. Both hands over her mouth, lest she scream and reveal herself to be a feeble woman, she got to her feet and rushed back to the house to call 999. What if he was dead? What if she had lost her 'best man in the world'?

She could hardly bear to consider the possibility as, after twenty years of prevaricating, he had eventually agreed that they could be married, so that she would inherit the widow's portion of his sizable private pension, should – God forbid – anything happen to him first. Now, she was having to consider just that possibility and, more trivial but just as important, how she would explain to all her respectable neighbours that they were not married at all yet, just living together.

The telephone woke Falconer at twenty minutes past three in the morning and, as he opened his eyes preparatory to answering it, he became aware of a small body lying across his feet on top of the bed covers. How the hell did she get there? he thought, as he spoke blearily into the mouthpiece. 'Whoozat?' he croaked, hoping that, even at this hour, it was a wrong number, and he could just hang up and go back to sleep.

'Bob? What the hell's happened at this time of the night – what time is it? God, it's past three.'

On the other end of the line, Bob Bryant, the desk duty sergeant from the police station in Market Darley, advised him that there had been a 999 call concerning an attack on a resident of Fallow Fold which could prove to be murder. 'I don't have a lot of details, but there's an ambulance on the way and, as Doc Christmas lives in the village itself, I've rung him as well. Perhaps you can get on to Carmichael and see if he can be ready to go with you, if you pick him up on the way.'

Castle Farthing, where Carmichael lived, was about seven miles from Market Darley, and then it was another five miles or so to Fallow Fold. It would be most convenient if Falconer could pick up his sergeant on the way. 'Have you got a name and address for me?' asked Falconer, now wide awake, and glaring at the small furry body on his bed.

'Rose Tree Cottage, Ploughman's Lays, almost directly opposite Doc Christmas' place. The name's Schmidt.'

'Schmidt? As in the German name?'

'As in "the Schmidt house is at the end of the garden",' replied Bob, reviving an old joke within the station.

'I'll wake Carmichael and be straight on my way.'

After ending the call, Falconer continued to gaze at Monkey for a few seconds longer, appraising the slimness of her body, and its ability to slip between bedroom door and doorframe while hook and eye were still in place. What a waste of time using those had been, he thought, and determined to get bolts to replace them. He'd like to see her outwit those. And just where were his socks, he'd like to know? And his tie?

As soon as he was out of bed, he dialled Carmichael's number, and waited for the shrill tocsin to wake one of the famously good sleepers in the household.

In Ploughman's Lays, in Christmas Cottage, an old family dwelling that had passed out of family hands for the better part of a hundred and fifty years, and then rebought by its present owner, Dr Philip Christmas apologised to his wife for her being woken at such an ungodly hour, and reassured her that he was only going across the road. As FME, he was required to attend all cases of suspicious death and, although this hadn't yet been confirmed, it certainly sounded like it would be.

Back in Castle Farthing, the ringing of the phone had caused Carmichael to sit bolt upright in bed and mumble, 'But it wasn't me, Ma, honestly!'

'What are you doing?' asked Kerry, his wife, sleepily. 'You'll wake up the kids if you start going on in your sleep. And get the phone. It's driving me mad.'

Carmichael reached automatically for the phone, now that Kerry had confirmed that that was where the irritatingly intrusive sound was coming from, and discovered Falconer on the other end of the line, urging him to get up, get dressed, and wait downstairs for him to call for him. They were off to a possible suspicious death in Fallow Fold.

'Whaa'?' mumbled Carmichael, still not quite free of his dream of malfeasance in his mother's eyes.

'We've got a call-out, you turnip. Get up! Now! Throw

some water round your face and don't go back to sleep, whatever you do.'

'Orright, sir. See you.'

As the sergeant stumbled out of bed, the slight commotion had wakened their house guest, Mulligan, and he ambled into the bedroom to see if there was anything going on that might interest him. Delighted to find his temporary master awake and just getting out of bed, he jumped up, immediately knocking Carmichael back onto the mattress.

'Gerroff, you daft dog!' he hissed, and rose again to fumble for his trousers, for he slept in his underpants.

He had only one leg in the garment, and had lifted his other to insert it, when Mulligan tried again to interest him in a game of, well, anything, so long as it was fun, and took place somewhere warm. Carmichael lost his balance, did a really accomplished little dance on one leg, hopping up and down the room. He finally lost the battle just before he reached the dressing table, at which point his head won the race, and the corner of the piece of furniture raised quite a lump on his forehead, accidentally dislodging Kerry's pot of loose face powder.

'Look what you've done now, you stupid mutt,' he hissed, sitting himself up, dusting the 'wild rose' tint from his head and face, and getting the second leg of his trousers on while still on the floor. It simply wasn't worth the risk of perhaps a matching bump on the other side, to rise to his feet again, at this juncture.

Mulligan, by way of apology, loped over and began to lick the blood from Carmichael's face, only to receive another telling off. 'If you get any of that on the carpet or bed, Kerry will skin you alive. Leave it alone, Mulligan! Bad dog! Anyway, that's a very unacceptable thing to do, to lick someone else's blood. What sort of a dog are you anyway? Did no one ever teach you any manners?'

'Whatever's going on down there?' Now Kerry was

awake again. They were both for it, now, if he didn't think fast.

'It's only the dog, come to see what's going on. I'm afraid he knocked your face powder off the dressing table, but I'll clear it up when I get back, and pick you up another one as soon as I can. Go back to sleep.'

Kerry subsided under the duvet, and Carmichael crept quietly down the stairs, Mulligan at his heels. As they reached the living room, the pups smelled the presence of the huge dog, and began to make high-pitched howling noises of distress.

In a complete panic, lest he disturb the whole family, Carmichael grabbed the canine colossus by the collar and rushed him out of the front door and on to the front door step, where he would not disturb the pups any more, but Carmichael would have a chance to put on his socks, shoes, and tie, which he still had in his hands.

For the next few minutes, he hoped he was not observed for, to anyone who did not know what had preceded the present situation, he would appear to be getting dressed *outside* his own home, and in the middle of the night, too.

As soon as he had sorted his footwear, sitting on the step, Mulligan landed across his lap with a sigh, to watch him tie his tie. 'Gerroff, you brute. You can come with us if you're a very good boy,' he whispered, and the dog replied with a whine of contentment, and immediately began to snore.

That is how Falconer found them when he pulled up outside the cottage, sergeant sitting on door step, huge animal sleeping across his lap. 'Why on earth have you got that big lummox with you?' asked Falconer, getting out of the car to investigate.

Before Carmichael could answer, Mulligan had woken up the instant he heard the voice of his beloved from Christmas, and bounded across to the inspector, nearly flooring him as he leapt up to lick his face, while Falconer struggled to escape this noisome and dribblesome embrace.

'Because he wanted to come, all right?' Carmichael finally replied, rather shortly, and determined not to end the statement with 'sir'. 'We'll take my car, and he can go in the back. If you want to leave him behind, I'll let you get him back indoors ... sir.'

The ambulance racing towards Fallow Fold was full of long-servers, who disliked having their night duty disturbed for anything less than a three-car pile-up. As it approached the entrance to the village, the driver snapped on the lights and sirens with a savage glee. If someone wanted to disturb their night for something that might turn out to be trivial, he was determined that a number of other people were going to be disturbed with him.

He wouldn't usually use the sirens without due reason, unless they were rushing to get through traffic before the chip shop closed of a lunchtime or evening, but this call-out, so far from their station had, somehow, annoyed him.

His act of black humour did cause some commotion inside many of the residences, waking the sleeping residents suddenly, to a sound that could only mean bad news, and causing many of them to immediately de-bed and grab for their dressing gowns and slippers. This was a village, after all, and one always wanted to be first to load a new item of news on to the mighty, but invisible, means of communication that was the grapevine.

Mabel Wickers was one of the first to hear the monster roaring into their midst, being one of the village's lighter sleepers, and was into her slippers and pulling on her ancient candlewick dressing gown before she was properly awake. She wasn't one for having to 'come to' slowly, and was out of her front door before anyone else except Doc Christmas.

She stood by the roadside, watching and waiting for the emergency vehicle to pull in to sight, so she would know which way to go, to be first with the news. She didn't have long to wait, for the ambulance drew up outside Rose Tree Cottage just a minute or two before she came out of her front door (which was in the side of the house; hence the property's name).

Madison Zuckerman was also quick off the mark, only to find that Duke was not snoring at her side, as she had expected, but was sitting up in bed, in a pose that suggested careful listening. 'There something bad happening,' she stated, identifying the noise that had roused her, and Duke nodded his head in agreement. 'We'd better go and see what's happening, honey,' she suggested, and they both rose to go and have a very British 'nose'.

'Couldn't ya sleep, honey?' she asked, as they trooped outside. 'Thought it would take a bomb going off to rouse you.'

'Guess I'm just gettin' older, that's all,' he replied, pointing next door, outside which stood an ambulance, its staff getting out of the vehicle, to be met by Mabel Wickers in 'nosy old lady' mode.

Right out on the edge of the village, Martin Fidgette's sharp hearing had caught the wailing tones and, when his shuffling and low curses at not being able to find his clothes in the dark roused Aggie, he explained that there was something going on further into the centre of the village, and he was going to go and find out what it was.

'Someone's already bothered to come all the way out here and deface my poor car. Who's to say they won't come back and do something else?' he asked, rhetorically. 'I want to find out what further mischief is afoot, before trouble comes back to our door. I can't afford to pay for any further gratuitous vandalism.'

Aggie sighed monumentally, and lifted her feet out of

bed to the floor. 'Wait a minute,' she exhorted him, 'and I'll come with you. I don't see why I should be left out, and I'm certainly not riding my bicycle at this time of the morning. My lights aren't working properly, and you promised you'd look at them yesterday.'

'Cut your cackle, woman, and get a move on. I don't want to be last on the scene.'

Antoinette Chateau awoke elegantly, as she did everything else in life, and lay in bed for a few minutes working out whether she wanted to know what was going on or not. Eventually, she decided that it was best to know what was abroad this night, and slipped on a pair of soft leather moccasins, before gathering a fashionable leather coat and going outside.

If it was something else nasty, maybe France *would* be a safer place for her. She had always considered an English village to be the most tranquil of places, but she was terribly unsettled about what had happened during the night of vandalism, and was having a really deep think about whether she was actually living in the right country.

The Dutch couple slept on peacefully, having consumed another few of their 'funny' cigarettes and, in Black Beams, the Maitland home, not a sound was to be heard. No one stirred. No one woke.

Doc Christmas was, by close proximity, the first official on the scene, and was pleased to be able to inform Heidi that Ferdie was not dead, merely unconscious, due to a sharp blow to the head with the inevitable blunt instrument.

'It's still a crime,' he informed her, 'although thankfully not a fatal one, and the police will have to attend to take statements, but at least you still have your partner, and I'm sure he'll be up and about again in no time.'

'He is best man in world,' she stated tearfully, relieved

that there would still be time for her to claim her widow's pension in due course. 'He is mine man – best in world – and I am worrying so much about him.' In her highly emotional state, she had lost a little of her grip on the language of her adopted country.

'Don't worry about him too much. If you want to wait around, I'll be going to the hospital to see him settled in, and you can come with me if you want to. I don't think you should be driving with you being in shock, but you can come back with me afterwards, when I come home to get ready for work. What do you say to that idea?'

'*Ich frage danke schon, Herr Doktor*. Thank you for very kind offer. I go now. I hear ambulance, and voices at front of *Haus*. I explain.'

The paramedics took over the examination of Ferdie's prone body, as Heidi moved off to face up to her responsibilities with what she guessed was a posse of neighbours, eager for news of more dastardly nocturnal deeds in their midst.

While the crowd had waited, there were various speculations as to what could have happened at Rose Tree Cottage.

'It's probably one of those love crimes,' was the opinion of Dale Ramsbottom who, with his wife Sharron, was one of the last to arrive on the scene. 'You know how hot-headed foreigners can be.'

'That's the French, with their crimes of passion,' contributed Mabel, more knowledgeable than he on the habits of other nationalities.

'Them bastards never seemed the sensitive types to me – the Germans in general, I mean, not those two.' This was Duke Zuckerman, troublemaking as usual.

'What do you mean?' asked Mabel, spotting the seeds of xenophobia in his statement.

'Oh, you know, just the war and everything. Can't say as I've ever known any other Krauts though, so who am I to judge?'

'Quite right, Duke. Now shut your mouth, and give your brain a chance to work before you open it again,' his wife admonished him with a grim face. 'No point in causing trouble where there ain't any. It could by any sort of domestic accident, for all we know, or even a heart attack. He's a big man, that Ferdie, and he might be prone, for all we know.'

Lionel Dixon merely observed events from the front window of The Retreat. It simply wasn't in his nature to join a ghoulish gathering like this. He preferred to keep his distance, and wait for someone to phone him with the actual details.

At this juncture, Heidi appeared round the front of the house and made an announcement that Ferdie had been attacked while waiting to trap anyone bent on any more damage to property, and that the police had been informed, and were on their way.

Carmichael's venerable old Skoda was indeed full, with two detectives in the front and a huge dog in the back; a huge dog that was determined to insinuate himself into the passenger seat to sit with his beloved.

'Will you keep that dog under control, Carmichael! He's managed to get his head halfway between the seats, and my trousers are absolutely soaked in dribble.'

'You control him, sir. I'm too busy driving. As it is, if I want to put on the handbrake or change gear, I'll have to give him an elbow in the snout, and I'm not so sure he wouldn't take a chunk out of me. It's you he wants to get to, but it's not just your space he's taking up, you know.'

'It's only *my* trousers he's slobbering all over, though, isn't it? I don't see why I should have to turn up at a new crime scene with dribble all over my trousers, and no believable explanation.'

'There's nothing I can do but stop and let you get in the

back with him. I can't drive like this; it's not safe,' stated Carmichael sternly.

'You can't do that,' replied Falconer, with anxiety in his voice.

'I shall have to. And if you don't agree, sir, I shall stop the car now, and refuse to drive any further. I do not want to be involved in an accident just because you won't sit in the back of my car. Now, move it! With all due respect. Sir.'

Falconer moved it, having been left no choice in the matter, and Mulligan was thrown into paroxysms of absolute euphoria at his arrival. Here was the nice man who had cuddled him every night when it was so dreadfully cold. The least he could do now was return the favour, and give his face a good licking, into the bargain, to show his gratitude for deeds past.

When they reached Fallow Fold, the crowd, which was now beginning to break up, at first, took Carmichael to be the superior officer. Granted, his tie might have been askew, and his shoes badly tied, but the damp and dishevelled scarecrow who got out of the back of the car looked more like someone who had been taken into police custody, rather than an officer of the law.

Doc Christmas was flabbergasted when he saw the state of Falconer. Both men had approached him, neither speaking nor looking at the other. 'Lovers' tiff?' asked the medic, sarcastically, then added, 'Or is this a case of domestic violence? What the hell happened to you, Harry? You look like a tramp. You hair's all over the place, you seem to be wet, and your clothes are so rumpled it looks like you've been hauled through a hedge backwards. And why are your trousers soaked through? You're surely not suffering from incontinence at your tender age.'

'He'll tell you tomorrow, Doc,' stated Carmichael, trying hard to suppress his mirth. 'Let's just say it's a shaggy dog story that'll keep until the morning.'

Falconer said nothing, merely reaching to straighten his tie and remove his handkerchief from his pocket in order to scrub his face, in a vain effort to remove the appalling smell of the dog's saliva from his nostrils.

'I gather Mulligan's back,' said Christmas, being well aware of Falconer's enforced stay at Carmichael's home over the festive period. 'I'll say no more.'

A two-man SOCO team had been summoned, and it did not take long to wrap up the details of what had been a distressing, but not murderous, assault on the now-hospitalised Ferdie. Falconer spent the whole time hoping that the doctor would offer him a lift home, but his pleading glances cut no mustard. Doc Christmas had promised to take Heidi with him when he left for Market Darley, and Falconer smelled so bad, he simply didn't want to be confined in a car with him.

'We'll stop in on mine before you go home, sir,' Carmichael volunteered generously. 'Then you can have a shower, I'll lend you something clean to go home in, and then you won't stink out your lovely Boxster.'

That was about the best thing that could happen before morning, and he agreed grudgingly, with the promise that Carmichael would keep the Hound of the Baskervilles off him as he left the house. He simply wasn't up to any more 'free love'.

The journey back to Castle Farthing proved to be not so exciting as the journey to Fallow fold, however, as Mulligan was quite exhausted after the delights of being reacquainted with his old room-mate, and slept the whole way back in the back seat, stretched across Falconer's legs, snoring, farting, and drooling happily, while his 'mattress' did its best not to breathe through its nose.

As the one-headed Cerberus slept the sleep of the innocent, Carmichael evidently had something on his mind, and asked, in a voice loud enough to be heard over

57

the noise, not only of the old car, but over the snoring coming from Falconer's lap, 'I'm thinking of having a tattoo done. What do you think, sir?'

'You're thinking of doing *what*?' Although Falconer had heard perfectly, he couldn't quite believe the content of what he'd heard.

'Getting a tattoo. What do you think?'

'Where?' was Falconer's first question, for knowing his sergeant, it would probably be something horribly visible, like a spider's web on the back of his neck, and that would not be a comfortable sight for any victim of crime, or witnesses, they might have to interview.

'In that place just off the Market Square,' replied Carmichael, oblivious that the import of the inspector's question had gone right over his head, not even stopping to ruffle his hair.

'I meant where on *your body*,' retorted Falconer, clarifying the matter by emphasising the last two words.

'Somewhere private that I'd rather not discuss.'

'Well, at least that's a relief, but knowing you, you'll catch blood poisoning from a dirty needle – or worse.'

'Can that really happen, sir?'

'Most definitely, and has on many occasions.'

There was a short silence while Carmichael brooded on this in the driver's seat, then he indicated that he had changed his mind by piping up with, 'I don't fancy risking that. I don't like hospitals, so maybe I'll get some temporary ones that wash off, and make do with those.'

'But nobody will see it anyway,' replied Falconer, logically. 'No one will know it's there.'

'I will!' was Carmichael's final word on the matter, but at least it didn't sound like he was going to mutilate his body and risk his health over one of his little fads.

As the inspector came downstairs at Jasmine Cottage, fresh, if dressed rather eccentrically in enormously over-sized clothes, he noticed that the pups had got over their fear of the monumental dog, and he was giving them, in turns, rides round the living room, slumped over his great snout.

At the door, he paused for a few moments to share his thoughts on the current disturbances in Fallow Fold. 'I don't like this one little bit,' he confided. 'A night of very personal destruction, and now an attack on a resident. The portents are not good, and I smell evil in the air. You mark my words: we're not finished with that village – not by a long chalk.'

His return home didn't improve his mood, as Monkey had evidently encouraged the other cats in further destruction of paper goods, and his *Radio Times* was a pile of shreds on the sofa. There had been yet another raid on his peace of mind by the Phantom Paper-Shredding Gang, and there was not a thing he could do about it, as all the suspects were currently slumped, wrapped in the arms of Morpheus.

With a long-suffering sigh, he mounted the stairs, determined to get as much sleep as he could before morning, and deal with anything other than his repose, when he rose. Things might not look better in the morning, but at least he wouldn't feel so ill-used.

Chapter Six

Sunday – Duty Hours

When Falconer arrived in the office the next morning, DC Roberts was conspicuous by his absence and, although this was not a rare occurrence first thing in the morning, he nevertheless rang down to Bob Bryant – still on duty – to see if there had been a phone call to warn them of his tardiness to report for duty.

'No, and there won't be,' said Bob enigmatically, then explained, 'He was the victim of a "Jelly" avalanche yesterday afternoon.'

'I beg your pardon, Bob. He was what?'

'He was in the office on his own, and Superintendent Chivers himself decided to do one of his snap spot checks, Saturday being his favourite day to try to catch officers napping. Well, he caught Roberts a good one.

'When he opened the door of the CID office, Roberts was sitting with his back to the door, his earphones in, bopping away and singing along to the music. He didn't even hear old Jelly come in, and the Super was able to sneak right up on him and put a hand on his shoulder, before the lad became aware that he wasn't alone.'

'Oh, my God! What did the old sadist do to him?'

'He's only gone and put him on traffic today and, as you know, there's one of those huge car boot sales going on in the Market Square. He'll be lucky to get out alive, what with the stallholders and the punters all milling around at the beginning and the end, cars and vans everywhere, all either trying to get the best parking place, or trying to get out before anyone else. Still, it'll teach the lazy little tyke to be a bit more dedicated to his job, and maybe make him grateful to have one at all, especially in CID.'

Falconer ended the call, chuckling. What stern words from him could not achieve, one brief visit from Chivers had brought about in one fell swoop, and he shouldn't have any more problems with the young officer for at least a couple of weeks. Maybe later he'd go down and watch him directing traffic, just for a laugh.

Neither Falconer nor Carmichael was supposed to be anything but on-call today, but the inspector had come in to instruct Merv Green and 'Twinkle' Starr on the events of the night before. They could go back to Fallow Fold and do a bit of door-to-door enquiring; see if anyone had any titbit of information that might help identify last night's attacker or, indeed, the vandal responsible for the first night of surprises.

Carmichael, he had directed to stay at home, unless called in. There was no point in both of them turning up in the office early, when both of them were rostered merely to be ready to respond. The office would survive well without them, as Sunday was a very quiet day, and Falconer's home was only a short way away should anything of note occur.

On his drive home, he made his slow and careful way through the edge of the Market Square, his spirits lifted by the frantic figure in the middle of all the action, arms waving maniacally, red in the face from blowing his whistle. It served Roberts right that he should be punished by such a vigorous duty.

Then he remembered the enormous amount of clearing up he had to do in his own home, and the trip to the DIY store to buy bolts for all his doors, and his spirits swooped again to their former nadir of the night before. He was already too fond of his new charge to consider handing her over to a cat rescue society, and was coming to terms with the fact that he'd just have to be one step ahead of her for the rest of the time they spent together. If only his other pets weren't so easily led.

He'd have to give her a little more positive attention; she was probably disturbed by her change of home, and needed to know she really belonged. Sometimes Falconer could be naïve beyond the bounds of belief, although he hadn't penned her up when she first arrived by locking the cat flap, like many a new owner would have done.

He somehow knew from the first moment that she jumped on to his shoulder, that she'd find her way back, now she'd met a whole crowd of new cohorts, wherever she wandered. That cat looked as if it were with him to stay. She had, at last, found her home.

At least he wasn't suffering the troubles of some of his colleagues in the force, with a wife, unhappy at his necessarily extended working hours, and children who had more or less forgotten what he looked like, and always took their mother's side in an argument.

At least he wasn't involved in a messy and heartbreaking divorce, like some he could mention – men who forgot that a family needs care and love, and not just a pay cheque at the end of each month. He was one of the lucky ones. To his mind, cats didn't leave you, or run off with another owner, although they could cause a great deal of trouble in one's life when they put their minds to it.

He had a happy, if temporarily disrupted, existence, his sergeant was deep in marital bliss, and it looked as though there could be an announcement in the near future from PCs Green and Starr. Roberts was just a drifter, and would probably be as happy on his own on a desert island as he would be in the ear-splitting din of a nightclub. He'd just fit in wherever he landed, and he rather hoped that his DC would find some direction in his life, soon. It might give him more incentive to concentrate on building his career with the police.

It was a philosophical but contented detective inspector who cleared up after his pets and took another trip to buy the unexpected necessities of little bolts from the DIY store that day.

In Fallow Fold that morning, Marilyn Maitland had woken late, having left Melvyn downstairs the previous evening to pursue his toot. These were getting longer and longer, and more frequent, and she surmised that he was getting itchy feet again.

They had, for long, lived under life's radar, never registering for tax or declaring themselves in permanent residence, always moving on when it looked as if someone might be about to blow the whistle on them. There was always someone, everywhere, who either worked for the government, had a grim streak of justice in them, or just a spiteful streak that led them to tell tales out of class.

They had got by through Melvyn's usual wheeling and dealing, but they'd been in Fallow Fold for longer than they usually stayed anywhere, and the jewellers, junk shops, and antique dealers for quite a radius were getting familiar with her husband. They'd have to head for territories new before long, and it was to this that she attributed Melvyn's unusually frequent and high consumption of alcohol.

She had known the personal Skid Row he had been headed for the previous evening, and had absented herself to the bedroom again, where she kept a secret stock of wine in her unusually deep knicker drawer. Melvyn would never think to look there, and he was always too bleary and hung-over after a night on the tiles to notice a corkscrew, empty wine bottle, and glass upstairs. Just in case, she always put these tell-tale signs in her wardrobe, out of his line of sight.

She had consumed a bottle and a half of red herself the previous night, before falling, helter-skelter, into a deep,

64

alcohol-induced slumber, and was not surprised when she found the other side of the bed empty when she awoke, heavy-eyed and muzzy-headed.

Melvyn she located slumped in an easy chair in his study, a picture of an old reprobate and lush. He must have slid down the back of the chair when he passed out, and his long grey hair was splayed up behind him on the chair back.

He had obviously been sick as well, for there was dried vomit in his unkempt beard, and down the front of his checked shirt. There was mud on his boots, which he hadn't even bothered to take off, and grass stains on the knees of his disreputable ancient jeans. What on earth had he been up to during the night?

Unaware of what had taken place at the house next door during the hours of darkness, she wasn't too worried, and dismissed his condition from her mind. It wasn't the first time she'd found him like this, and it certainly wouldn't be the last. Anyway, she felt pretty dreadful herself, and betook herself off to the kitchen for a large mug of strong coffee and a reviving dose of liver salts.

Lionel Dixon, the Schmidts' neighbour on the other side who had watched the nocturnal event from his front bedroom window, came downstairs to find another envelope on his hall mat, the double of the anonymous one he had previously received. This, he picked up with right fore-finger and thumbnails, as if his hand were a pair of human tweezers. He felt so queasy, he thought that if he actually touched the thing, he might throw up.

He knew what it would contain, and temporarily hid it from himself behind the clock on the sitting room mantelpiece. He'd need some ammunition in him, before he could stomach perusing the evil therein contained, and made his way to the kitchen in a state of nervous tension.

Yes, he knew he should have opened it immediately; he

knew who had put it through his letterbox; and he knew he should confront the sender but, now, as once before, he simply lacked the required backbone. He was also honest enough to realise that he would never show the letter to the police, but there was one person he could consult, and maybe call off the dog of war.

There was one other from whom he could seek advice and information in a subtle way and, steeling himself to open the second letter, then add it to the first in the secret drawer of his bureau, he approached the telephone with more than a little misgiving.

Between these two troubled households, in Rose Tree House, Heidi was contemplating her forthcoming interview with the police. In her panic of the previous night, she had forgotten all about Ferdie taking his air pistol out with him, in an effort to brand the prowler in an unmistakable way.

It had come to light, however, as soon as Ferdie's inert body – dead, in her mind's eye – had been turned over, and there it had been, underneath his considerable and solid gut, where he must have dropped it, just as some person unknown had dropped him.

Would Ferdie be charged with carrying an offensive weapon, even though he was on his own property, and only in pursuit of discouraging any further vandalism to private property? Would she get into trouble for knowing what he was doing, and not discouraging him from carrying out his foolhardy plan of action? Would she be upbraided for forgetting to point out that they were not married, and her name was actually Heidi Laux, not Schmidt? If only she had thought to remove the weapon, none of this would be happening.

Granted, Ferdie would still be in hospital, but he hadn't actually fired the gun, and no one would have known anything about its existence, had she not thoughtlessly left it outside, in her panic. *Mein Gott*, was it an offence here, to actually own such a thing without a licence? She didn't know the answer to any of the questions that were ranging through her mind, and she was in turmoil.

This was the first time they had run into any trouble, other than the usual kind of xenophobic behaviour in which some British people felt obliged to indulge, and she was scared, not just for their position within (or without) the law, but also for how serious Ferdie's injury was. She would visit him during the course of the afternoon, and hoped to find him in not too bad a way.

During the afternoon, there was much exchanging of gossip and conjecture in Fallow Fold, not least between regular members of the congregation and choir of the Church of St Mary Magdalene. Coffee was always served from an urn at the back of the church after service and, this week, a larger number of people than usual stayed behind to sip and snipe.

Martin and Aggie Fidgette were, naturally, at the heart of this, with Martin as choir master, and his wife as a leading member of the choir. He was still in a fury about the price that had been quoted for the repair to the paintwork of his beloved old car.

It really was a toss-up, what with the excess on his premium, whether to claim and have the work done immediately and live with the higher monthly payments, or to stay as he was, and save up to have the work done. It seemed grossly unfair that he should be financially penalised for the wantonly destructive behaviour of unthinking and uncaring others.

It was he who started a hare running, with a racist remark that particular morning. Still wearing his choir master's robes, he stated, 'Bloody foreigners overrunning the village these days. Last night one of them got what he deserved, and who's to say that it wasn't another one of the devils that did all that spiteful damage the night before?'

'Martin!' Aggie upbraided him, shocked at his hate-filled statement.

'Well, there's nobody to say it but me in this place. Everyone else is so nicey-nicey, and doesn't dare speak their mind. It takes someone with my guts to bring everything out into the open, if these things are going to be cleared up, and not become regular features of the life of Fallow Fold.'

'I couldn't agree more,' added Duke Zuckerman. 'Where were they all in the war?' He could ask this question because Antoinette was not a believer, and therefore didn't attend services, the Dutch couple never rose before noon on a Sunday, and the Schmidts were otherwise engaged today, and did not attend as a regular event anyway.

'The French and the Dutch were hiding under the stairs from the Nazi jackboot, and it was only the British and the Americans who dared to question their right to rape Europe.'

'Shut up, Duke,' snapped Madison. 'Wrong time, wrong place!'

'I'm only saying what everyone else is thinking,' he retorted, with a strange gleeful grin on his face. 'Someone gave that Kraut what for, and I'm not exactly crying into my hankie.'

'No, but you are making a racist fool of yourself in front of half the village. Just can it, baby. You can vent your spleen in the privacy of our own home, when we're not on consecrated ground.' Madison was getting angry with her loose-lipped husband. This wasn't the way to make friends and influence people, and Duke should know better. Before he knew it, they'd be tarred with the same brush, even though they were native English speakers.

'The war's been over for well over sixty years. Poor

Ferdie wasn't even born when it happened. How on earth can you put him in the same category as those who were alive at that time? And most people who did what they did, did it because their survival depended on it!' This was the ever-sensible voice of Mabel Wickers. 'Live and let live; that's what I say.'

'You say what you like, Mabel. I simply don't trust foreigners.'

'Duke, I think it's about time we went home. You're not in a very sociable mood today, and I think we ought to be getting along, before you say something *I'll* regret.'

As the American couple exited the building, Dale Ramsbottom had the urge to add his two-penn'orth. 'Actually, I tend to agree with old Duke. Why should it always be our villages that the damned foreigners decide to settle in? I don't see them flooding into Castle Farthing, or Stoney Cross, or even Steynham St Michael. Why here? What've we got that other villages don't have?'

'Obviously not tolerance,' spat Mabel Wickers, and stumped out of the church in disgust.

'I think it's all our lovely social hobby circles,' opined Sharron Ramsbottom. 'There's such a wide choice of activities, you can keep yourself busy when you're retired, even if it is like us, in early retirement, and never be bored.'

'The war was nothing to do with the Schmidts or any of those others. But perhaps *we* should set up a branch of the Hitler Youth here, and then we could all go around and spray swastikas all over the properties of those residents who can't prove one hundred per cent Anglo-Saxon white lineage.' Aggie Fidgette was also feeling ill at the amount of hatred that had been generated by recent events, and deeply ashamed that her husband had been the instigator of this particular hate-fest.

Just a week ago, she would never have thought this sort of discussion even possible, let alone likely. Not only did she not really know her neighbours, it would seem that she didn't even know her own husband well enough to sense his secret bigotry.

When Mabel had huffed her indignant way home, she was surprised to receive a phone call from Lionel Dixon, asking if she would entertain a short discussion that he felt it imperative he have with someone whom he knew not to be a malicious gossip or rumour-monger.

This lightened her mood considerably, after the conversations and comments she had just heard – and in a church, of all places – and she agreed to let him pop over whenever it was convenient for him. There was nothing like a little flattery to boost the ego.

He arrived at her back door, which was furthest from the road, and out of sight of casual passers-by, about a quarter of an hour later, looking flustered and nervous, and he shot into the house almost before she could invite him to enter.

'What on earth is the matter with you, Lionel? You look like you're being pursued by all the hounds of hell,' she asked, after letting him settle in an armchair in the sitting room.

'I have something that has been preying on my conscience, and I wanted to ask advice as to what I should do. Should I just leave things as they are, or should I do what all my instincts dictate?'

'I'll get us a little pre-luncheon sherry, and you can tell me all about it,' she replied, heading for the decanter on the sideboard. 'Is this a personal matter, or does it involve others?'

'It's nothing to do with me,' he replied, a little too vehemently. 'But I do think it's something that ought to be … ah … regularised.'

'Here you are,' she said, handing him a small schooner of pale liquid. 'Drink this and get it all off your chest.

You'll feel better for it.' And so would she. It might wash away the nasty taste in her mouth with which the gathering after the service had left her.

Dixon was a master of prevarication, and he wrapped up his own, very personal problem, by disguising it as a matter of legality. 'What do you know about that Maitland couple?' he began. 'Only, I have some very serious suspicions about them, especially the chap.'

'Has he rattled your cage, Lionel?' asked Mabel with a wicked twinkle in her eye. She wondered if maybe Melvyn had insulted his sensibilities. Maybe he had called him an old woman, or even hinted that he was not as manly as a man should be. That would certainly drive Lionel to a savage fury of self-protection and protestations.

'I won't reveal my sources for these suspicions,' he brayed, self-righteously, 'but I happen to believe that the man is guilty of tax evasion on a grand scale, and not just income tax.'

'That's a pretty stiff accusation, old ... boy,' she replied, managing to avoid calling him an old woman. 'Where's your evidence?'

'Oh, I have my sources, as I said before, but they will remain anonymous,' replied Lionel, slyly. 'I just don't know what to do about it. What would you advise?'

This was getting as dirty as the comments on incoming foreigners had been at the church, and Mable's feeling of discomfort was returning. Draining her glass hurriedly, glad she had only filled small schooners, she rose slowly from her chair, saying, 'I should look to the dictates of your own conscience. This isn't anything to do with me, but if it leaves you uncomfortable, knowing this, then get it off your chest. Just don't ask me to ratify what you decide to do.'

Lionel also rose, having heard enough to reassure him that the decision he had made earlier was the right one, and he snuck back to The Retreat, much more at ease in his mind, not even noticing the stiffening in Mabel's manner. He should have known there was a logical and easy resolution to the harassment that he was suffering. Hit his tormentor where it hurts; that was the ticket!

In Castle Farthing, the focus for the whole day was preparation for the baptism of the Carmichael household's three children in the village church on Wednesday evening. The couple had not wanted it to be during the day on a Sunday, perhaps even during a service, because, with his vast and party-animal family, it would degenerate into the rocket-fuelled booze-fest that had so unnerved the inspector. It would be a small, intimate affair.

He had asked special permission for the lady vicar of Shepford St Bernard – Castle Farthing not having its own vicar at the moment – to conduct a candlelight service for him, close members of his family, and a few carefully chosen friends and fellow residents of the village. The two boys, Dean and Kyle, had an inset day on Thursday, thus upsetting their usual bedtime would not be a problem, and baby Harriet could sleep on a clothesline, thank God.

At work, he had been full of the plans he and Kerry were making to ensure this was an unforgettable family affair, but had been rather distracted over the last couple of days, due to giving Monkey away, and the forgotten and completely unanticipated arrival of Mulligan. Today, however, he was full of good ideas, sitting with Kerry at the dining table, ticking things off lists and making new ones, when old ones were finished with.

'The cake will be brought over on Wednesday afternoon,' Kerry informed him. 'Auntie Rosemary's friend has already finished it. She's just giving it a little more time to dry out and set the icing. Auntie and I will be working on the food during the morning, and again, after the cake arrives, and we'll take it straight to the village hall. George Covington's offered to help with that, taking it in the back of his van, so that should go all right.

'The Yaxley twins are taking care of the music, and your brothers are setting out the tables and chairs for the short supper afterwards, and we'll hope to be done and dusted by ten. I've got the old christening robe that Auntie Marian gave me before she ...'

At this point, Kerry gulped, and suppressed tears. There had been a tragedy involving her godmother in the recent past, and she still could not bear to talk about her. 'Sorry, Davey. I've got the gown, and the old goffering iron, so our Hattie's going to look like a right little princess.'

'That's my girl. Whatever would I have done if I hadn't met you?'

'Met someone else instead,' Kerry teased him with a watery smile.

'Not in a million years. You're the only one for me, and you know it,' he replied, planting a kiss on her head. 'We were fated to spend our lives together, so no arguing!' Davey Carmichael had never been happier in his life.

Having fitted the last little bolt, Falconer took his seal-point Siamese into the privacy of his bedroom, and sat him down on the bed, to give him a good talking to about his position in the household. 'Now, look here, old chap; you're the founding member of this feline gang, and you've got to exercise some discipline. You know neither of us likes to live in a muddle, but that's what you're letting that monkey, Monkey, turn the place into. Get a grip, and dole out some discipline, so that things can get back to normal. Got it? Good!'

As his speech had unfolded, he had leaned closer and closer to Mycroft, and the cat's reply to his plea was to give him a look of withering Siamese disdain, as if to say, his owner would never understand the power of the pure-bred feline charisma that Monkey exuded, and to lick him affectionately on the nose. 'I hope that was in lieu of a spoken agreement,' said the cat's owner, and smiled at the lithe creature, who had once lived as an only cat, in a much less rumbustious atmosphere as existed in the house now, and had never complained about it. Or misbehaved. Before.

Chapter Seven

Monday

As Falconer dropped his briefcase beside his desk on Monday morning, the telephone shrilled loudly in the empty office. He didn't know whether to expect DC Roberts back today, or whether Superintendent Chivers would keep him on traffic duty as further punishment. Carmichael he expected at any minute.

'Good morning,' he spoke into the mouthpiece of the instrument. 'Market Darley CID. Inspector Falconer speaking. How may I help you?'

A vaguely familiar voice identified itself as Wanda Warwick from Shepford St Bernard, and his mind visualised the white witch he had met in the course of his last case. 'I'm calling again about Bonnie Fletcher – you know? – the one who just seemed to disappear into thin air?'

'I remember. You mean she hasn't turned up yet, or got in touch?'

'Not a word,' Wanda replied, anxiety in her voice.

'And you said "again". Have you phoned the station before?'

'I know it was only Saturday, but the officer did say I'd be contacted before the end of the day, and I heard nothing that afternoon, and not a dicky bird yesterday; and I know the police are a twenty-four hour service now, so I was a bit surprised.'

'Did you get the name of the officer you spoke to?'

'It was a DC Roberts. Why? Is there a problem?'

'Not for you, Ms Warwick. If you could drop into the

station, we can officially record her as a missing person, and start a search for her. Are you sure she hasn't just gone on holiday?'

'Bloody long holiday, then. It's been over six weeks, maybe more, since I've seen her. I've even phoned her office, when I saw her job being advertised in the local paper on Saturday, and they just said that she'd broken the terms of her contract of employment, so was deemed to have left their employ.'

'Does she have any relatives you could get in touch with?'

'None that I know of. I know her grandmother left her the cottage, but I've never heard her mention any family. I think there'd been a bit of a serious falling out, if you ask me, and she'd cut all ties.'

'I'll wait for any details you can give us about her, with maybe a recent photograph, and I'll get things moving our end. Thank you for following up the lack of response to your previous call, and may I apologise on behalf of the Market Darley police.'

The inspector sighed in exasperation as he ended the call, and became aware of Carmichael's mighty lurking presence behind him. Turning round, he started, and asked abruptly, 'Good God, Carmichael! What the hell are you wearing?'

The DS looked down at himself, and shrugged his shoulders in incomprehension. It was a little early in the year, temperature-wise, for his personal 'sartorial silly season', and he gazed in puzzlement at his navy jacket, white shirt, and sober tie. Whatever was the problem?

'The jeans, Carmichael, the jeans! Where are your suit trousers?'

'Oh, those. I'd forgotten I'd even got these on. They're Mulligan's fault.'

'What did he do, eat your matching trousers?'

'No, but he certainly ate something. I came down this

76

morning, not fully dressed, because I heard this dreadful noise of an animal in distress, and it turned out to be poor old Mulligan choking on something.

'Just as I got downstairs to him, to see if I could help, he chucked up all over my trousers. I was worried sick, because there seemed to be a squeaking noise coming from his throat, but when I looked at what he'd brought up, it was only the squeaky toy that Mistress Fang used to act out being mother to, before she whelped. For a moment, I actually thought he'd eaten a puppy.

'So that was the end of my trousers, until they've gone to the dry cleaner's. You could never just sponge out anything that Mulligan brought up. He'd just had his breakfast and, boy, was he loaded. Never mind! That's the joy of pets, isn't it, sir?'

'Yes,' agreed sir, even during his current hiatus in peaceful living.

'All ready for Wednesday?' asked the DS, suit trouser crisis already forgotten, and a proud and happy smile on his face, at the thought of the forthcoming celebrations.

'Of course I am, as godfather-in-chief to all three,' Falconer replied, 'but at the moment I find it necessary to hunt down DC Roberts and scrag him, yet again. Do you know if he'll be in today, or whether he'll be continuing his little holiday in traffic?'

'When did he transfer to traffic?' asked Carmichael, who had not been party to the story of Chivers' surprise weekend raid on the station.

'When "Jelly" caught him in here listening to his music and chair-bopping, with an almost empty desk in front of him. One of Chivers' surprise Saturday raids. It's all right; I'll just give Bob on the desk a ring, and see what's happening.'

'What's he done now, if you're after his hide?'

'Do you remember that white witch from Shepford St Bernard? Wanda Warwick was her name?'

'How could I forget her?' replied Carmichael. 'She was a pretty spooky person. Why?'

'Apparently she called the station on Saturday morning to say that her friend Bonnie Fletcher was still missing. If you remember, she was worried about her when we were working a case in the village. And the young woman still hasn't turned up. Ms Warwick phoned it in, and spoke to Roberts, who promised she'd be contacted again later in day, but she's heard absolutely nothing from him. Why the cloth-head just couldn't have taken down the details himself, I've no idea.'

As he explained the situation, he was rustling through a collection of little notes and notelets on Roberts' desk that were the only things that marked it out as 'in use'. 'Here's his note about the call, with a piece of used chewing gum stuck to it. Lazy, thoughtless little devil. This is just about the end. He's a complete waste of space.'

'Who is?' asked a voice from the door, and the subject of Falconer's contumely shuffled into the office clutching his right side, and groaning.

'You are, and what the hell's up with you?' asked the inspector, not feeling very charitably disposed towards the department's newest member.

'Bloody awful pain in the side. I was all right when I woke up, but it came on when I was parking. It just comes and goes, and I've no idea what it is, but it sure is a pain in the arse, and I've had it for days now.'

'Language, Roberts! Have you seen a doctor?'

'I saw enough of them to last me a lifetime since I moved here. I seem to spend all my time in the hospital, and I don't plan on returning there any time soon.'

Flopping into his chair, he groaned with pain, and exclaimed, 'God, it hurts bad!'

Falconer sent him to the canteen for a cup of tea and a couple of paracetamol, to see if he could ease the pain before his superior set about him for his lack of attention to detail and devotion to duty. He could hardly discipline the man if he was physically suffering. Not only would it make Falconer feel like a heel, but Roberts wouldn't take in any of it, because he was distracted by how bad he was feeling.

Half an hour later, now immersed in paperwork, Falconer became aware of the sounds of a siren approaching the station, and looked out of the window to see an ambulance just pulling up outside the main entrance. What the hell was occurring? Was there someone in the drunk-tank from the night before, who needed urgent medical attention?

He soon found his answer, as DC Roberts was carried past on a stretcher covered with a snow-white sheet and groaning with pain. Within a few minutes, Bob Bryant had already tapped into the station grapevine and ascertained that the DC was suffering from a burst appendix. Falconer's wigging would have to wait some time before he could vent his spleen on the officer, who was on his way back to the hospital for his third stay since joining the department: third case, third emergency.

After all, he could hardly stand in the operating theatre beside the surgeon and give him a good verbal going-over, could he? He'd be unconscious; and no nurse would tolerate the bollocking of one the patients in her care, from a senior officer standing at the sick man's bedside, while he lay in his bed of pain.

But at least he hadn't been swinging the lead, which the inspector had begun to think he was. He supposed he ought to feel bad, but he just didn't. That young man was capable of spending most of his working life in hospital for one thing or another, and still come out at the end of it with a respectable pension.

When he returned to the office, Carmichael asked, seemingly with no relevance to anything Falconer could think of, 'Do you watch *South Park*, sir?'

'Never heard of it. What's that got to do with anything?'

'Nothing, sir.'

For the rest of the day, the inspector was to keep hearing people talking about someone called Kenny, but no one of that name worked at the station, and he remained puzzled as he went about his daily duties.

That Monday in Fallow Fold, at Black Beams, panic reigned supreme. There had been a telephone call during the morning from the income tax office. Luckily, Marilyn had fielded it, found out who was calling, and told the caller that there was no one by the name of Melvyn Maitland living at the address, and she was just a local cleaner who had been called in to clear up the house after their departure.

No, she admitted, with her fingers crossed behind her back, she didn't know where they'd gone; she just knew that they weren't coming back. She had no idea who their anonymous informant had been, and she didn't know the man whom they were calling at all. She had just got a message through her door with an envelope of cash, asking her to make everything look tidy for the next tenant.

She didn't know whether the letter was from the owner or the tenant, but a small amount of money was enclosed, there were instructions for where to find the key, and she had gone round there to do it, as she had been paid for the job.

Promising to pass on any information, and pretending to make a note of the phone number, she gave a false name and address in Carsfold, and rushed off in great anxiety to Melvyn, to tell him that someone had rumbled them and turned them over to the authorities.

Melvyn had not quite recovered from his night on the tiles the night before, and was just emerging from the shower, looking a little bit, but not a lot, more human.

'Don't worry about it,' he advised her in a laconic voice. 'It's happened before, and it'll happen again. Do you remember that time we had someone round snooping – that big place up north – and we both hid under the grand piano, because no one could see under there from any of the windows? Ah, those were the days, eh?'

'No, they bloody well weren't, Mel. I thought you were glamorous when I met you, with your hippie looks and laid-back attitude to life, but for me, it's been one long nightmare.'

'Sure, you've had fun. Admit it: it's been exciting,' he countered.

'Maybe for you, but I've just spend my whole married life in fear of exposure, and I don't find that very relaxing or enjoyable. We have to settle down properly. I'm getting too old for all this skipping around. I need some stability.'

'Sure, you do,' mumbled Melvyn, still towelling his thick, long grey hair and long untidy beard. 'You'll get over it once we find somewhere new, and the game starts again. I'll sit down at the computer now, and find a likely area for us to head for; somewhere we've never been before, where no one will know us from Adam.'

'You do that. I'm going for a walk!' stated Marilyn, grumpily, and left him to his own devices.

'If you don't like the heat, you should stay out of the kitchen,' he called after her. 'You should've stuck with that nice boy from college. You'd probably be contemplating a nice retirement bungalow by now, and be taking holidays in Spain, like all the other people who never really achieve anything in life.'

'At least they achieve a happy life, which is more than I've had. We're just like criminals on the run all the time, and what have you actually achieved? You're no spring chicken, we own no property, and we have no kids to enjoy. Tell me, just what have you achieved?'

'I've never been bored, and that's something not a lot

of people can say.'

'No. You've never been bored, so that's all right then, isn't it? Melvyn Maitland has never been bored, so all's right with the world.'

'And I've never been boring, either!' he stated with absolute conviction.

'Oh, I don't know. Your life's always run to exactly the same pattern, really: get established somewhere, live undetected, do a lot of dodgy dealing, then move on, no further forward and no better off. You are boring and predictable, and now it's happening again. And exactly where do we get the money to move on with?'

'That's all in hand. Don't worry your pretty little head about the money.'

At this, his wife made her final exit down the stairs and out of the back door to seek some private solace. She, at least, had one friend in the village to whom she could turn in times of trouble, and she made her way there with as much haste as she could muster, knowing she would receive tea and sympathy, and maybe more solace than she had reason to deserve, if she were lucky. But cruel fate had more in store for the hapless couple before the day was out.

Mabel Wickers, a little further down Ploughman's Lays, was also in a turmoil of mind that Monday morning. She had slept badly, owing to what Lionel had not only told her, but had hinted, at their pre-luncheon sherry the previous noon.

While noting what he did say, she had also been able, to a certain extent, to read between the lines, and she had an idea there was more mischief going on in Fallow Fold than was identifiable on the surface. There was something, so far, secret, going forward, and there was something she could do which might act as a catalyst.

Settling down at the dining room table, she

contemplated a blank sheet of paper, put her mind into cunning mode, and began to word her short missive. This should, at least, generate some interest, and it might flush everything else up to the surface, so that life in the village could be resolved, and return to its old, peaceful pace of life. She would remain anonymous, however, as she wanted to keep herself at a distance from such activities, and remain aloof as to the final outcome.

Within half an hour of DC Roberts being taken away by ambulance, the two detectives made their way to the hospital, realising that the situation, for Roberts, was once again, serious.

There was no sign of the patient in A&E, but a passing nurse enquired, and told them that their colleague had been prepped and was already in theatre, due to the grave nature of his problem. There would, unfortunately, not be a doctor or surgeon for them to converse with until the patient was in the recovery ward.

'You can take a seat, if you like, and wait, but I think it'll be some time before there's any news. Let me make a note on his file of your contact numbers and, if there's any news before you come in again, I'll get someone to ring you, and keep you up to date with his situation.'

'Come on, Carmichael,' said Falconer, after they'd sat for a while with a cup of truly disgusting lukewarm coffee. 'Let's get ourselves off to Shepford St Bernard, and just have a look round Bonnie Fletcher's property. We can call in on Ms Warwick while we're there, and save her a trip into Market Darley. Then we can get the details of where she worked, and see if there's been any contact, maybe suppressed, with her colleagues.'

Wanda Warwick was not at home when they called at her cottage, but they found her in Robin's Perch actually looking for a fairly recent photograph of its owner. They had intended just to have a look round the back and through the windows, but found the back door wide open, giving the place a bit of an air.

'Hello,' she called out to them. 'I thought I'd see what I could find for you, and whether there was anything that might indicate that she intended to go away. I haven't found anything so far, but she's got an awful lot of mail.

'I was going to go through it before coming into the station, so that I could sort the wheat from the chaff, and only pass on personal mail, and not the junk.'

'That's unusually thoughtful of you. If you don't mind, we'll have a look round ourselves. We might notice something that might not mean anything to you, but might give us an indication of what her intentions were. Of course, once she's officially reported as a missing person, we can have a forensic team look over the place. They're very good at picking up clues that are invisible to the naked eye.'

'I've cast her tarot cards several times since she's gone missing,' Wanda informed them, 'but they're just a jumble. It almost looks like they're empty readings, with nothing to tell me. I don't like it. I don't like it at all. Sometimes I get this terrible empty feeling that she's just not there any more: that she's dead.'

'Don't worry yourself unnecessarily. If she's alive, we'll find her; you can rest assured of that,' Falconer reassured her.

'And if she's dead?' asked the worried woman.

There was no answer to that.

Bonnie Fletcher was posted as officially missing later that day, and a local radio appeal went out, as did a piece in the local paper, with a reproduction of the most recent photograph to be found in her home.

Her workmates said they had not heard from her since the day she had, presumably, disappeared, when she was looking forward to a hot date that night, but would give no details, merely promising to give them a blow-by-blow account after the event. There had been no contact or sightings since.

When the members of the Bridge Circle turned up at The Retreat that evening, the curtains were open, but there were no lights on inside. There was no answer to their rings and knocks at the front door and, one by one, they gathered on the garden path, wondering what on earth could have happened to distract Lionel Dixon from his beloved bridge.

He may not be the sociable sort, or even very interesting, but he was a demon card player, and they thought it highly unlikely that he would just miss a meeting without either a courtesy telephone call, or an urgent matter that distracted him to the extent that he had forgotten what day it was.

One of the more adventurous members went round to the back of the house, and called down the side of the property that the back door wasn't locked, and that they'd better just check inside to see that he hadn't taken a tumble, or something similar, and was actually lying in there, undiscovered and injured.

That was a fantastic idea, to have a bit of a gander round his home without him there to restrict their movements, and all the members piled in at the back door, full of curiosity to look for Lionel in any of the rooms that they had not previously been admitted to – just in case he was unconscious and in need of help.

The little tables he used for the meetings in the dining room were not laid out as usual, and the card boxes were nowhere to be seen, and there had been no tasty little titbits prepared in advance in the kitchen for their delectation. In fact, there had been no preparation inside the house at all for this evening's meeting, and it looked as if he had been gone for some hours, as he wasn't to be found anywhere in a distressed state, not even in his wardrobe or his hitherto private underwear drawers.

Eventually, when the majority of them had finished poking and prying where they had no business to be, a note was spotted propped against the mantel clock and, on opening, proved to read: *Had to go to Mother. Urgent. Sorry.*

'Who'd have thought he still wore boxer shorts,' was one comment, as they left the property, having searched every cubic inch of it for their missing leader. 'Do you think we ought to lock the back door and take the key?'

'He left a note, and never mentioned locking up, so I guess we just leave things as we found them. He'll be back, as soon as this crisis, whatever it is, is over, and he won't thank us for moving as much as a mote of dust in his very private home.'

'Why didn't he leave the note stuck on the front door, then?'

'Because anyone could have seen it, and he might've been robbed.'

'That's his look out. If he is, it isn't our fault.'

The matter was deemed to be a storm in a teacup, and the meeting was rearranged to take place in one of the other member's houses, with all of them nipping home to find something to add to the evening's snack table, at present like Old Mother Hubbard's larder – absolutely bare. They wouldn't be robbed of their bridge by this minor, if unusual, setback.

Chapter Eight

Tuesday

Tuesday's post brought surprises for more than one address. In Black Beams, Marilyn, who usually opened the post to save Melvyn the task of yelling obscenities at some of the stuff that came through the letterbox, actually yelped when she opened, first, a form to apply for a television licence, and second, an application form to register for the privilege of paying council tax, as their offices had been informed that Mr M. Maitland was now in permanent residence.

Both authorities would be grateful to know the date from which Mr Maitland had been eligible to pay for these essentials, and had enclosed a preliminary bill from yesterday's date, with projected payment for the next twelve calendar months, and a box in which to state the date on which they moved in to the property.

'Mel!' she practically screamed. 'Someone's really got it in for us! Look what's come in the post! First, that phone call from the tax office yesterday, and now these!'

Perusing the communications, his face blackened with fury, and he almost spat, when he spoke. 'I know who's responsible for this, and I intend to do something about it before the day is out.'

'Don't do anything rash, Mel. We've got to get out of here unobtrusively after all.'

'I'll be discreet, my little treasure, and you can get packing right now. We'll go tonight. I know exactly where, now. No one will find us, I promise you. We'll be safe again, where this devil can't drop us in it again. Just don't ask me what I'm up to until we're ready to go,'

Marilyn found his mood rather frightening, but was quite happy to be left to her own devices, too. There was a mort of plans to be made yet.

Falconer also found something of interest in his office morning mail. For once, first class post had lived up to its claims. Granted, it was an anonymous letter, and he usually viewed these in a very dubious light, but this one had the postmark of Fallow Fold, and the printing was legible, the spelling impeccable. This could be a genuine tip-off, that someone knew what was rumbling under the surface in the village, and its arrival only confirmed his own misgivings.

The letter consisted of only five words, but they were very telling words, as he read: *I KNOW WHO DID IT*. Now all he needed to do was find out who had written the letter, and what they knew, and he might have a clue as to who had been on a vandalism spree in the small community, and had escalated their campaign of anti-social behaviour to ABH.

He'd go out there with Carmichael, to see if he could flush out his anonymous informant, but it would have to wait a little. It wasn't as if anyone had been murdered, was it?

Duke Zuckerman had been restless since the disturbances in the village and, on Monday afternoon, announced to Madison his plans to return to the States immediately. He claimed to have been very unsettled by what had happened in their ideal little village, and needed a return to his roots to settle him down.

'But why will that help, honey?' Madison queried. 'We moved here to get away from all the stuff that goes on over there.'

'Maybe I just miss the kids, and the ball games, and the

88

food. Maybe I'm missing the culture I was brought up in, and all my good old buddies, and this English crap's making me feel a bit hemmed in,' was his vague reply.

'You do what you want to do, Duke. I've got plenty to keep me occupied here, so I shall hardly notice you've gone – no offence meant, honey.'

'No offence taken. I'm glad you don't mind. I just feel I need to get away for a while. I'll phone the airport now, see if I can get a last-minute deal.' Madison truly would not miss him much, except for the taking out of the household waste. She had a great deal of work to do on the quilt she wanted to exhibit this year, and not having to wait on Duke's every whim would leave her a lot more time to attend to this.

Also, he'd been acting kinda weird the last few days, and it made her feel kinda jittery and uncomfortable, as if he knew a secret she didn't. A bit of time apart would probably do both of them a power of good.

Maybe she could join him for a week or so before the kids were due to come over, and then they could go back with the kids at the end of their English vacation, as planned. This change of schedule would be advantageous, and would give her something to look forward to sooner before the kids actually came over.

Meanwhile, in the Maitland household, Melvyn was stamping around like an enraged bull, pulling paperwork out of his desk and filing cabinet, and trekking off to the kitchen where he stuffed it into the fiery interior of the range at such a rate that smoke poured out of their chimney, making anyone who saw it wonder what sort of cold person lived there, to need a fire on such a lovely warm day.

Marilyn packed personal things upstairs on her own. Melvyn's possessions she just stuffed into boxes without a care about folding them. He was the cause of all her troubles, so why should she care about him? And what was the point, anyway?

Her own things, however, she packed with considerably more care, making sure they were rolled or folded to cause the minimum of creasing, and placed into suitcases or holdalls in good order. Her clothes were all that she had in the world, and that world was not of her own making and, lately, not of her own choosing.

Why should her possessions suffer because Melvyn was off on another of his gypsy adventures? She'd had enough of the whole thing. Her life had ceased to work some time ago, and it was high time she did something about it.

While her husband continued to simmer and thump about on the ground floor, she made a couple of calls on her mobile phone – she had to have some privacy. She wasn't just another of Melvyn's possessions, after all – and thought her secret thoughts.

The only blessing about this flit was that the furniture came with the house. They didn't own a stick of that, either. Melvyn had been the original rolling stone who had gathered no moss whatsoever, not even a bed of his own. At least the travelling would be light.

The Book Circle meeting at Sideways that evening was unusually well attended, and Mabel Wickers was flitting about like an overweight fairy, making extra pots of tea and coffee, and raiding her larder for more biscuits and sweetmeats to keep her guests occupied.

Most of them had come not to discuss the current book being read, but to chew over the recent events in the village, and accusations were rife as to who was responsible for the wanton damage that had been done, as well as the attack on their German neighbour.

Opinion was divided. Many of them had noticed the deteriorating mood of Melvyn, and had spoken, even if very briefly, with Marilyn, about her husband's increased drinking, and were tempted to blame him and his explosive temper.

A few, for some reason as yet unfathomable, thought that the culprit could live within the membership of the Amateur Dramatic Circle but, when asked why, could only come up with a weak response that hinted at jealousy on the part of someone in that group; that they were outside, what the speaker considered to be, the 'inner circles'.

'I've been speaking to that doctor's wife, Stella Christmas, and she's in the AmDrams. She thinks it looks like the work of a spiteful child, and we know what a load of spoilt children that lot are, fighting about who does this and that, and who gets the best part, or costume,' offered Sharron Ramsbottom, who had joined the circle during the dire winter weather, due to the lack of opportunity to even get into the garden, but hadn't managed to stick it out for more than a few weeks.

'It's not like any one group was targeted with the damage, is it? It was more a random attack on group members in general, and not *one* of those poncy actors had any trouble whatsoever.'

'What about the attack on poor Mr Schmidt?' asked Mabel, puffing through with yet another tray of tea and coffee.

'That was probably more of the same thing, except Mr Schmidt was waiting for the culprit, ready to defend his property. I hope he doesn't get into trouble with the police. It's only right that you should be able to stop people damaging your stuff.'

'Hear, hear!' cheered Dale Ramsbottom, who had come along to support his wife; not that he read such things as books, but he was feeling at a loose end this evening, and anything was better than what was advertised as on the box. 'An Englishman's home is his castle.'

'But Mr Schmidt isn't an Englishman,' Mabel threw

into the conversation.

'That's beside the point, Mabel, and you know it. Those two work tirelessly to present their garden as a showpiece, and I don't see why he should have to sit around and just let someone trash it.'

'Hear, hear! again,' spake her 'ever-loving'. 'If anyone had a go at my garden, I'd be prepared to give them what for. We'll just have to be extra vigilant, and try to keep a better eye on our homes and gardens.'

'And cars. But don't let Martin Fidgette hear you talking about cars. He's still absolutely rabid about what it's going to cost him to put right the paintwork on his.'

'But absolutely no vigilantes!' Mabel cautioned, collecting up dirty crockery, and wishing they'd all go home. They'd hardly spent ten minutes talking about their current read, and she'd like time to get back to hers, as she had neglected it of late.

Had it not been such a crashing bore of a volume, she'd have read it long before now. Maybe next month, she'd have a title ready for them, and hopefully, one that was a little less dry than the one they were currently critiquing.

If she kept her mind occupied, she wouldn't find herself thinking, again, about that foolhardy letter she had posted, shoving it into the post-box before she lost her nerve, and now wishing she had been a little more circumspect.

With no cognisance of the accusations about him that were being bandied about just across the road, Melvyn continued to rage around, calling down contumely on everyone in the locality, and hurling larger personal possessions no longer needed into the garden, to be abandoned.

At midnight, Maitland said he had some last minute business to attend to, and Marilyn sighed with relief to be out of his company at last. Three minutes later, there was a tap on the back door, and she answered it cautiously, just in case there was a last-minute hitch.

At one o'clock in the morning, a van pulled out of the drive of Black Beams and drove off into the night, unseen by any wakeful neighbour or insomniac early hours' walker.

Everything had gone to plan – well almost. There had only been one hitch, but there was no point in thinking about that at the moment.

Chapter Nine

Wednesday

The following morning, a van load of boxes was stored in a lock-up garage on one of the more maze-like areas of Carsfold, and a couple, each with a grip holdall, walked to a bed and breakfast establishment, where a prior booking had been made the day before.

They would not be staying long, and claimed to be on a touring holiday, but had been caught out when their car broke down the previous day. They had managed to get to Carsfold by local bus, and would wait for their vehicle to be repaired before they moved on. They seemed a nice older, respectable couple, and nobody gave them a second glance.

By lunchtime on Wednesday, Falconer found he could not bear Carmichael's presence any more. The sergeant was cock-a-hoop at the forthcoming events of the evening, and if he wasn't singing or whistling, he was dancing on the spot and waving around his arms to music that only existed inside his own head.

Excited, hyperactive kids had nothing on Carmichael. He could outdo their irritating behaviour without having to make any effort whatsoever, due to his uncurbed, natural exuberance.

Eventually, the inspector's patience snapped with an almost audible 'ping', and he yelled, completely out of the blue, as far as his sergeant was concerned, 'Get out of this office! At once! Go home and do something useful! Kerry could probably do with another pair of hands! I simply can't think straight with you capering around like a drug-fuelled tarantula.'

Then, to take the sting out of the tail, as Carmichael wasn't doing anything wrong, just being happy, he added, 'And have you got that Mulligan entered for the three thirty at Newbury, or does he need re-shoeing? When's he booked in with the farrier?'

'Ta, sir! And don't be silly. It's the two thirty at Chepstow he's running in,' replied Carmichael, with a facetious answer that trumped Falconer's ace nicely. 'Now, promise me you won't be late tonight. We can't start the proceedings without the most important guest of all; the man who delivered our little Hattie, can we?'

'Who's dog-sitting?' asked Falconer, forever a practical soul.

'Paula Covington from The Fisherman's Flies. She doesn't reckon they'll be very busy tonight, with all this malarkey at the church and the hall.'

'That's kind of her. Now, get along, and let me get my head straight, or I'll get nothing useful done all day.'

This was like the school bell for the sergeant, and he capered out of the office and down the corridor towards the stairs, like a hulking great schoolboy finally let out of school for the day, whooping with glee so loudly that he made Bob Bryant on the desk visibly jump.

'Harry sent you home, lad?' he asked, when his nerves had settled down.

'Yes,' agreed Carmichael, giving one final 'woo-hoo' of unbounded joy.

'Good!'

'Christening, this evening, Sarge.'

'Good!'

Bryant was just about sick to death of hearing about the ruddy triple christening, and this final insult to his nerves, as Carmichael cheered himself out of the building, had put the tin lid on it for him. Although, he supposed he'd have to suffer a confetti shower of photographs for the next few weeks. That was all right, he just wouldn't pay attention.

How Falconer stood the young man's unbridled enthusiasm every working day was a mystery to him, although he knew that there was no harm in him. He could just be wearing, at times, with all that youthful energy to dissipate. The complete opposite of Roberts, he was.

Mabel Wickers sat in her sideways-on house and fretted. Perhaps she shouldn't have sent that letter. With hindsight, what did she actually know for sure? Only what she had been told, and that might just be a tissue of lies, inspired by nothing more than natural antipathy or prejudice against a less conventional lifestyle.

She'd been drinking far too much coffee, and rather more sherry than was good for her. She felt so uneasy that she decided, on the spur of the moment, to go to her friend's house in Market Darley, and spend a day or two there. Maybe Lena could advise her, or at least point her in the right direction.

Mabel knew, of course, that the right direction was to go straight to the police station to report that it was she who had written that anonymous letter, but she wasn't ready for confession yet, and needed someone stronger than herself to set her on the path to righteousness.

She left on the afternoon bus, thus missing the fact that, that evening, no lights glowed in either Black Beams, or The Retreat, and that there had been no sign of movement in either house since the day before; which was a pity, as so much might have been changed, if she'd only stayed behind to face the music, earlier than she was now about to do.

Even more soppy sentimentality and enthusiasm entered Falconer's office when Merv Green and Linda Starr slipped in briefly, to announce that they were getting

97

engaged. Carmichael, of course, would have been ecstatic for them but, due to his unscheduled absence, it was the inspector who had to endure almost half an hour of proposed wedding arrangements, cakes, dresses, honeymoon destinations, and venues.

At that point, his patience reached the end of its leash, and he found himself promising to meet them for a quick drink after work, to raise a glass to the future. 'Mind, I can't stay long,' he said. 'I've got to get over to Castle Farthing for the Carmichael baptisms. I am chief godfather, you know.'

'No worries, sir,' said Merv, with a grin. 'We've been invited as well, so we could meet half an hour before the kick-off, in Carmichael's local, then we'd be right on hand for when the ceremony starts.'

'Good idea, Green. I'll see you in The Fisherman's Flies later, then.'

'It's a date, sir.'

Falconer, unusually for him, left the station on time that day. He wasn't sure what sort of state the house would be in when he got home, and he needed sufficient time to do his toilette, before turning up at the Carmichael thrash, as guest of honour. At least the baptism wasn't being approached in the same way as the sergeant's and Kerry's wedding, which had been a themed fancy-dress affair, with everyone in pantomime costume.

He believed that tonight's celebrations would be wholesome and quiet, respectful and grown-up, and that he need have no fears of those dreadful Carmichael brothers spiking his drink, and making him look a fool, again. Carmichael was an extremely moral and upright character, but the same could not be said for the rest of his tribe – and he used the word 'tribe' consciously.

Fortunately, nothing in his household, now he had fitted bolts to all the doors, was shredded or destroyed – with the exception of three juvenile rats, who had suffered an unplanned post-mortem on the kitchen floor, and made his stomach heave, as he went out to put on the kettle for an after-work cup of tea and fetch a plastic rubbish bag.

Arranged around the soft furnishings, five cats slept in blissful innocence. Who? Did what? Not us! That must have been some other cats, when you were out and we were taking a nap. He could hear their reaction to his interrogation already, and knew it would be a waste of time.

Wearing some rather natty spearmint-coloured rubber gloves, and clutching a handful of paper towels as an extra barrier against the squishiness of the various inside bits of rat that had found their unfortunate way outside their hosts, he cleared up the mess, disinfected the floor, and sat down to drink his Earl Grey before jumping into the shower.

As he soaped and rinsed, and shampooed and rinsed, he imagined the uproar that probably held sway in the Carmichael household, the preparations only being made more difficult by the pups and dogs, as Paula Covington probably wouldn't arrive for her dog-sitting duties much before they left for the church.

Then he remembered that they still had Mulligan as a house guest, and laughed out loud, which had the unfortunate effect of him getting a mouthful of shampoo bubbles. Coughing and spluttering, he realised that Carmichael could even interfere with his peaceful existence from as far away as his own home.

He dressed carefully in his best Italian suit, and his favourite pair of shoes, that he had purchased in Venice, at a little place on the Rialto Bridge, confident that he would arrive home as immaculately attired as he left it, his duty done, and the thought pleased him.

It had been quite a while ago that Carmichael had originally asked him to be godfather to the boys. It must have been when he was going through the official adoption process, before young Harriet had been born. Here, he winced, as he remembered the baby's delivery, with only midwife Falconer on duty, the arriving-little-girl's father having passed out on the sofa.

The subject had been dropped for a long while, but been revived now and again, and it was only on their last case together that Carmichael had had the get-up-and-go to do something about arranging a date for this momentous family event.

Granted, Castle Farthing didn't have a resident vicar any more, and that was an obstacle that meant arranging anything, had to be thought of when there was actually a local vicar in view, but he was glad that it would, at last, be laid to rest, and he wouldn't have to worry about it any more, popping up out of the woodwork, like an evil spirit, to taunt him.

As he got into his Boxster to leave for Castle Farthing, the sun was shining, and all was well with the world.

In the bar of The Fisherman's Flies, Falconer found the two out of uniform PCs already arrived, and having a drink with the Carmichael brothers. And sisters. A quick tot-up revealed the presence of Romeo, Hamlet, Mercutio, Juliet, and Imogen, some of whom had been school contemporaries of both Merv and Linda.

Taking a deep breath to inspire courage, he strolled, as nonchalantly as he could, over to them, and bade them good evening. The eyes of both Merc and Rome lit up when they identified who had greeted them. Here was game indeed; a victim on the hoof, as it were.

With an easy innocence, Imogen, catching the looks of her brothers, offered Falconer a drink, then winked at the others behind his back. This was sport that none of them had anticipated and, here it was, delivered right into their hands. They didn't need to speak about their plans, as they were almost telepathic when confronted with a target for mischief.

Juliet engaged him in conversation, playing on how lovely it was that such a fantastic couple as Merv and Linda were finally getting together, while Merv moved over to the dartboard with Ham and Rome, the chief trouble-maker. They'd had a thoroughly good time playing with Davey's boss at the wedding, and this could be a good opportunity to repeat the experience.

Of course, had their mother and baby Harry been in the bar, they would never have dared to plan such an outrage. But they weren't. So they did. As far as they were concerned, Falconer was an innocent abroad, and deserved to be taken advantage of by the natives. All it took was a wink to Juliet, Ham, and Imogen, and the plan was set.

Falconer had ordered a half of black-and-white Irish, as sufficient fluid and alcohol to sustain him before the service, and sipped cautiously at it as the talk settled on weddings, past, present, and future. The inspector had no awareness whatsoever that, when distracted by one of the Carmichael sirens, the other was slipping a tot of vodka into his glass.

Peanuts were proffered to distract the taste-buds and increase thirst and, before he knew what was happening, another half-pint glass sat in front of him. 'Go on,' urged Imogen. 'It's only a pint, with the two of them put together. No harm in them at all.'

The innocent abroad took her at her word, and his drink continued to be added to, tot by tot, until Merv, Romeo, and Mercutio finished their game of darts and re-joined the others at the bar. 'Quick brandy for the road?' asked Romeo and, before Falconer could refuse, the glass was already on the bar in front of him, and it seemed churlish to refuse.

Downing it in one, like the Carmichaels, he went to leave his place, leaning on the bar top, and found that his legs both wanted to go in different directions and leave him in the middle with no means of holding himself up. He was also bemused to find that the bar now seemed to be located on a sea-going craft, and that the floor heaved gently up and down with the movement of the waves.

He found himself supported surprisingly gently, one brother at each side of him, and towed across to the church, like a stricken boat being led to shore, wondering why he felt so peculiar when, to his certain knowledge, he had consumed no more than a pint of Irish and a shot of brandy.

On entering the church, the double candles that he saw created a tremendous urge in him to giggle, and he was staggered to see how many sets of twins were in attendance. A huge Carmichael leaned down to him and mouthed words that he was unable to understand, so he just smiled in a friendly way, and waited to be led to his seat.

He also beamed at Rev. Florrie, the vicar from Shepford St Bernard, as she seemed to want to have a look at him, too. Never had he been so popular. What he didn't hear, however, was the urgent conversation being conducted at the back of the church in whispers.

'What did you do to him, Rome?' hissed Carmichael, his good humour on its last legs since the entrance of the inspector, evidently in an advanced state of inebriation.

'We just slipped him a couple of Russians, to ease his nerves,' replied Romeo.

'He's clearly the highly strung, nervy type,' added Mercutio, 'so we thought we'd take the edge off things for him.'

'We were only doing it for you, Davey, boy,' concluded Hamlet, beginning to feel worried at the expression, redolent of storm clouds, that was gathering on his brother's face.

'If you've spoilt this for me, then I'm finished with the lot of you. Your childish little pranks may seem funny to you, but this is one of the most important days of my life, you little toads.'

A shadow was cast across the whole group as Mrs Carmichael senior joined them, and asked in no certain terms, what had happened. 'It's these clowns, Ma. They've only gone and spiked Inspector Falconer's drink in the pub, and now he's almost legless. He's supposed to be chief godfather. What the hell are we going to do?'

Ma wasted no time on words. Grasping Romeo and Hamlet by an ear each, she dragged them painfully outside to give her instructions for saving the day, and she would brook no argument.

Amidst the candlelight and spring flowers that lent their atmosphere to the chill inside of the church, Falconer stood straight and tall, as he repeated the age-old words. He renounced the devil and all his works, and he turned to the light, accepting the lit candle he was offered, although he held it in a somewhat wavering way. He stood for photographs afterwards, and smiled for the camera, as if there were nothing wrong.

What he did not do was appreciate how beautiful the old Castle Farthing church looked, bathed in the light of a multitude of candles, and decorated with flowers from almost every garden in the village.

The brigadier, who sat in the back row, was particularly furious, because his wife had positively raped his flower garden for their contribution to this display, telling him in a patient and logical voice, that such a severe pruning would encourage them to grow even better, and it wasn't often they had such an event in the village church, now they no longer had a vicar of their own.

Falconer kissed baby Harriet and patted the boys on the head, congratulated the parents, thanked Rev. Florrie for a beautiful and memorable service, and all this with a back-up squad of three Carmichaels.

When he had completed his formal duties in the church,

Ma Carmichael and two of her sons steered him outside and round to the back of the church, where he was gloriously and flamboyantly sick, before collapsing from the knees up. By now, he could decipher what was being said around him with much more clarity, and he listened to the conversation that was taking place above his spinning head.

'If I ever catch you little bastards doing anything so stupid and irresponsible again, I'll turn you in for assault and poisoning. That was the inspector you were fooling with. He's an important man, and he expected to drive himself home tonight. What if he'd actually managed to get in a car? You'd have been had up for manslaughter, that's what would have happened!'

'You actually brought your remedy with you, Ma?' asked Romeo, still amazed that his mother had saved the day for everyone.

'You bet I did, you little toe-rag. Now, let this be a lesson to you. You're not kids any more, and you can't go around playing foolish pranks on those with a position in society. You leave orf your childish ways, from tonight onwards.

'I don't ever want to hear again about you spiking anyone's drink. It's a bit more than a fall off a push bike these days, now you're getting on a bit. Most of your friends would have got into a van or something, and then driven into a brick wall – or something similar – and you'd be behind bars for the rest of your days. Act your ages, not your shoe sizes! This is the last time I'm going to tell you.'

Ma Carmichael, when there were celebrations in the offing, usually carried a battered old flask with her, which contained a magic potion known only to her, the recipe having come from her grandmother. No one else in the family knew what went into it, apart from tabasco sauce, but it could evaporate drunkenness for a period of up to an hour or more, before the recipient collapsed. It was a little of this that she had administered to the chief godfather in the privacy of the church porch, just before the service started.

She had sidled up until she sat beside him, told him he looked a little peaky, then led him away to somewhere they wouldn't be disturbed, now that all had assembled. Then she just held the flask to his lips. Falconer was so far gone that he sipped automatically, and didn't even think of questioning what he was drinking.

As she put her flask back in her capacious handbag, Ma Carmichael took a peek at her patient, and was pleased at what she saw. The inspector was now red of face, his eyes were starting out of his head, his mouth hung open, and his body had begun to twitch all over.

Sliding back to her own place, she smiled with pleasure. Once again, the old cure was working, and he should be good until after the dunking and name-calling. After that, he'd probably have to be removed from public view until morning, as the after-effects could be hair-raising and even more undignified than making an arse of oneself in public.

As soon as the baptismal service concluded, and she had had her little word with two of the main miscreants, she ordered them to take Falconer back to Davey's place and put him to bed. He'd be fit for nothing else before the morrow, and he'd need a good long sleep to get the various ingredients out of his system.

That only left her with one problem. She knew he had cats, and they would need feeding both tonight and in the morning. Grabbing Ham and demanding his van keys, she took a drive over to Market Darley. She knew where tonight's poor victim lived, and called in to see his next-door neighbour when she got there, explaining that the man next door had been taken poorly at a party, and wouldn't be home before tomorrow afternoon at the earliest.

The neighbour, being a conscientious animal-lover himself, and who had a key, promised to take care of the situation, and that she was to tell the stricken Mr Falconer not to worry one little bit about his charges. They would be well looked after.

Ma Carmichael was feared and adored by each and every one of her children in equal measure. She was a formidable woman who could cope with everything but spiders, and she felt she'd saved, not only Falconer's face, but Davey's celebration as well. All she had to do was drive back and mention that the inspector had been feeling unwell, and had retired to the cottage for a little lie down. The truth could come out tomorrow, as it inevitably would have to, when Falconer told what he could remember of the night before.

She'd deal with the irresponsible behaviour of her own brood in good time. Let them wait. Let them stew.

Even without the godfather-in-chief being present, the party removed itself to the village hall, and the celebrations got underway.

The hall was decorated, as it usually was for any village celebration, with balloons and streamers. Folding tables and chairs had been set out in a 'U' shape, and food, to which everyone present had contributed in some way, was set out on the tables, along with party hats and blowers – Carmichael couldn't resist such childish additions to any party.

The cake for the occasion was set in the middle of the short length of the 'U', and was, in typical Carmichael style, a representation of another of his passions. Not for him the traditional fruit cake iced and decorated with flowers. He had ordered a huge wheel of a cake adorned with five blue creatures of varying sizes; to whit, his family represented as Smurfs, for he had an extensive collection of the little blue people, collected over the years.

Small bunches of spring flowers also adorned the tables, and Rev. Florrie had brought over with her the DJ-ing twins who so enlivened parties in Shepford St Bernard, knowing that if anyone could make a party go with a swing, it was these two youngsters. They not only had an extensive collection of music, but could tailor it, at a glance, to suit the mix of people gathered to celebrate.

To start with, though, there were speeches from the proud father and the officiating vicar (in the absence of a certain godfather), and toasts to those newly enrolled in the Christian family.

Carmichael had bought a new suit for the occasion, there being a branch of outfitters in Market Darley that could provide for his unconventionally large build, and Kerry wore a simple dress of white cheesecloth, embroidered with bright flowers at the neck and the hem, and they both looked as if they would burst with pride.

The proud father, red of face and stuttering with nerves to start with, soon gained confidence, and gave a moving talk on how his life had changed since he had met Kerry, and how she, the boys, and now young Harriet, had made his life heaven on earth, ending with, 'and no man could ask for more, or be happier than I am today.'

There was a huge round of applause as he finished, and many an eye was filled with tears, moved by the simplicity of Carmichael's earthly treasures, which were people, and not worldly goods or money.

Rev. Florrie make a brief speech in which she thanked all those who had attended, explaining that baptisms were on the decrease, as were church numbers, and that it had been an honour and a pleasure to officiate at such a well-attended and happy occasion.

The highlight of the evening for some however, was seeing Carmichael dance for the first time. By build, he had unnaturally long legs and arms, but when these were released to react to the beat of music, no one was safe for a distance of several yards, and eventually other dancers just stopped to watch him.

He was lost in the music, and flung himself around with abandon and his eyes shut so tightly that, when the music ended, he found himself with an audience of just about every guest, some of whom were doubled up with mirth.

One of the twins took the microphone at this point, and announced that anyone on the dance floor at the same time as their host may consider wearing a hard hat, and even Carmichael could see the joke, having been videoed once, performing what Kerry referred to as his Downland Tribal Fling.

Falconer himself was totally oblivious to the small party that returned to the cottage for a bit more of the afterglow. He knew nothing about Carmichael looking in on him, to see that he was all right, and in the recovery position. He noticed nothing when Kerry threw a duvet over him, as he was collapsed on top of the bed, nor when she removed his shoes and loosened his tie. He slept on, innocent and un-assaulted.

After his unanticipated slug from Ma Carmichael's battered old flask, the next thing that Falconer was aware of was his face being washed, and he thought, for a second or two, that he was back in the nursery. But never had such a foul-smelling face-cloth been used on him before, and that moved him to open one sticky and encrusted eye, only to find that it was looking into another eye, but much bigger than his own, and rather bloodshot.

His second eye creaked open, and was immediately closed again by a voluptuous lick. This definitely wasn't any nanny he'd known! With a groan, as he moved his head, a plaintive whine assaulted his delicate hearing, and a pile of boulders crashed inside his head. If he wasn't mistaken – and he certainly could be the state he felt he was in – there was a dog with him, wherever he was.

Had he been involved in an accident? He didn't remember being anywhere where there was likely to be a landslide. It also didn't feel as if he were lying on the ground somewhere. It was soft underneath him, but a vile smell was assailing his nostrils, so maybe he had been injured by a chemical explosion.

At that moment, a thunderously loud voice broke into his reverie, and he identified what sounded like Carmichael with a loud-hailer booming, 'Morning, sir. Mulligan, we know you love him, but stop all this farting for joy routine. You'll gas the poor inspector, and he's only just back in the land of the living. Bacon and eggs, sir?'

Every item of information arrived in a rush. He was in Carmichael's house. He was in bed with that bloody dog again, his insides were about to explode like Vesuvius, and it would be impolite to let that happen in front of, let alone all over, his sergeant. There was half a thought in there that involved a christening, but his priority was to react to the word evacuation in all its meanings.

Rising almost vertically, the pathetic figure on the bed exited the bedroom with more energy than it had seemed possible it could contain, entered the bathroom with a howl like a screaming banshee, slammed the door behind it, and then made noises that made Carmichael's hair stand on end, while he considered that he might have to redecorate in there rather sooner than he had thought.

Chapter Ten

Thursday

A little later, a raggedy wildman sat on the settee in Carmichael's living room, twitching and coughing, as the house-holder encouraged him to finish drinking a black mixture from an egg-cup. 'You've got to drink it, sir. It's the antidote.'

'The antidote to what? What on earth did I eat at last night's reception to land me in such a state?'

'You never made the reception, sir. You barely made the ceremony, and you certainly didn't have anything to eat.'

'Then, what the hell happened to me? I feel like I've been excavated by a food processor, then run through a mangle.'

'My brothers, sir. They're what happened to you, but for now, it's most important that you finish this antidote.'

'But what in the name of blue blazes is it an antidote for? Snakebites?'

'My mother's cure-all panacea.'

'And what if I don't want to take it?' He was acting very childishly, and he knew it, but childish was how he felt.

'Then you'll be laid up for days. Just drink it. I'll hold your nose if you like.'

'You keep your hands off my nose. Hold your own, if you want something to do. Give it here!' Falconer grabbed the egg-cup and swallowed it in one, then retched, and wished he hadn't.

'Keep it down, sir. It'll do you good,' Carmichael

111

advised, watching him with anxious eyes.

Falconer sat, his face narrating the story of the struggle his insides were having to retain the tiny amount of noxious liquid, then he went a rather funny shade of mauve, took an enormous breath, and asked for a cup of coffee. 'By golly, that was good stuff!' was his only comment, as he smelled frying bacon from the kitchen, and suddenly felt on top of the world.

A few minutes later, he regained the power of coherent speech and said, 'I still don't know what happened, but if this marvellous feeling that has just infused my body is courtesy of something your mother did, then she's a truly wonderful woman. Now, what about some breakfast, and we can discuss what happened yesterday evening later. There doesn't seem to be any harm done.'

There was only one further moment of panic, halfway through a hearty and very unhealthy fried breakfast, when Falconer suddenly remembered his abandoned cats, but he was quickly soothed with the tale of Ma Carmichael's quick thinking and positive action. He would go straight home after he had eaten, having first checked his alcohol level with a breathalyser – property of Market Darley police station – and would join his sergeant as soon as he'd showered, changed, and begun to feel more like himself, and less like an animated scarecrow.

It was Stella Christmas, wife of Doc Christmas, that first suspected there might be something amiss across the road, and she voiced her anxieties that Thursday morning over breakfast. 'You know that Lionel missed Bridge Circle this week?' she asked her husband.

'You said he'd left a message about going to see his mother,' answered her husband, his mouth full of eggy soldier.

'I'm getting a bit worried about him,' Stella replied, her forehead creased in concern.

'He's a grown man.'

'But it's not like him to just disappear like that.' Stella was pressing home her point. 'You know how punctilious he is about everything? It's just so unlike him not to phone at least one member and get them to pass on a message.'

'Maybe it was an emergency,' countered Philip, drinking deeply from his enormous breakfast teacup.

'If it was an emergency, it would've been quicker to make a phone call than to write a note and prop it up tidily on the mantelpiece.'

'Has anyone seen him since he went away? I mean, he may be back, and just keeping himself to himself.'

'There were no lights on there last night. I made a point of looking, so that I could drop in today if he'd returned.' She'd got her teeth into things now, and Philip knew it was better to let her have her head than to try to talk any sense into her.

'I'll tell you what,' he suggested, 'you ask around and see if anyone's seen him. Ring his number, and knock on the door as well, and if you don't turn up an explanation, let me know. I suppose he could have had an accident, or something, while visiting his mother, and even be in hospital, waiting for someone to notice he's not around. He's so self-effacing he'd be likely to do something daft like that.'

'But he's also a stickler for good manners and detail.' Stella was determined to make a mystery out of it. 'If he was in hospital and conscious, he'd probably have got someone to call Mabel Wickers. He's as friendly, if not more, with her as he is with anyone else hereabouts.'

'Drop in on old Mabel as well, then. Now, I've got to get to work. You get digging, Poirot, and let me know what you turn up.'

Kissing his wife on the forehead, Dr Philip Christmas left the house, dismissing the matter from his mind, and having not the faintest idea what his wife's idle curiosity would turn up.

Stella Christmas knew her husband didn't take her worries about Lionel Dixon seriously, but she was genuinely perturbed. It was so out of character for the man not to dot all the 'i's and cross all the 't's, and to go away without a word to anyone, was decidedly out of character.

As she cleared away the breakfast things, she made her plans for the day. She could go next door to Sideways and have a word with Mabel, to see if he'd said anything to her about his mother. Then she'd ring his number on the telephone and, if there was no answer, she'd go over to the house itself and bang on the door.

A little peep through the windows wouldn't be amiss, although she knew that the Bridge Circle members had searched every inch of the property on Monday, as she'd been one of them. He may have returned in the meantime, however, and done something stupid, like falling off a stepladder while changing a light bulb.

If none of these actions turned up anything, she'd go off and do a little shopping on the village parade, see if she couldn't stir up a little gossip on her errands. After that, she'd be stumped, but at least she could let Philip know that no one knew where the man had got to.

But, hey up, she could call at Black Beams to see if the Maitlands knew where he was. She knew that Lionel and Marilyn had a friendship of sorts, and she might know more than anyone else, once pressed.

The owner of the Carsfold bed and breakfast still had the middle-age couple in residence. For a pair touring the area, they spent an awful lot of time in their room, and their car still didn't seem to be repaired.

He wasted no time worrying about that, though, for as long as they paid their way, they could stay till kingdom come as far as he was concerned. They were quiet, their needs were modest, and they didn't bother him. If only all his guests were so little trouble.

At her friend Lena's house in Market Darley, Mabel Wickers was unable to settle or relax. Her mind was in a turmoil about what had been going on in Fallow Fold, and she finally decided that it would be better for her to go back there, and get to the bottom of what was happening, then return to Lena's when she was in a calmer frame of mind.

She didn't see her friend many times a year, although there was not much geographic difference between their addresses, and she didn't mean to waste an opportunity to reminisce and have a laugh, because she was too preoccupied to relax.

She hadn't intended to stay long anyway, so she'd leave in the morning, after making arrangements to come and stay for a full week later in the year. She'd be back on the trail on Friday morning and, maybe, she ought to own up to sending that letter.

Stella Christmas considered the shops on the village parade. The post office and the hairdresser's were easy. She could call in for some stamps and then make an appointment for a cut; she was certainly due for one. The tearooms could provide her mid-morning break, and the rest would just constitute her shopping for the next few days, although she usually ordered her provisions online.

She could pick up bits and pieces from the mini-market, a few other bits and bobs from the general store, and make an enquiry on behalf of a non-existent friend for a property in the area at the estate agent's. If she used a low enough price range, they'd have nothing, and be none the wiser about the real reason for her visit – and she intended to be nothing if not thorough.

If she went into the bakery, the greengrocer's, and the butcher's as well, she could get some nice cakes for after dinner tonight, and the greens and meat for the Sunday roast, and that would be every establishment visited. If she couldn't pick up some gossip with all those calls, then her name wasn't Stella Christmas. And it was.

As the shops were just to the south of Christmas Cottage, she wouldn't even need to get out her little car. She could do the whole thing on foot, and if she didn't glean much, she could make some social calls this afternoon. Sometimes she got quite bored at home, which was the reason she had joined the amateur dramatics group. Learning her lines at least gave her something constructive to do.

It was a very warm day again, and she had no need for a coat, but her weather eye decided that there would be a storm arriving in the not-too-distant future. This gorgeously warm and sunny spell couldn't last for long; not in this country.

As she had no intentions of making any heavy purchases, she treated herself to taking her wicker basket with her, which always reminded her of childhood daily shopping trips with her mother – so it was with a light heart that she trotted the few yards necessary to reach the start of the retail establishments available to the residents of Fallow Fold.

A lot of the shopkeepers were in the drama group, so they wouldn't find it odd that she was rather chatty in a nosy sort of way, today. They'd probably just think she was extra loquacious due to the good mood produced by this prolonged spell of sunshine and balmy breezes.

Their establishments had been renovated from the shells of the old shops that had been, variously, corn merchants, ironmongers, feed and seed sellers, and outlets for local produce, and had been saved, by a grant from a heritage fund, from demolition and replacement by a soulless parade of modern shops.

There were black beams aplenty, and mullioned

windows, thatch and ancient tile, and they all wore striped, coloured awnings with pride. Their owners, in the main, lived in the renovated accommodation above the commercial premises, and formed a small community of their own within the larger community of the village.

The owner of the minimarket confided that he thought the Maitlands were on the fiddle, somehow. He didn't know what they were up to, but he had always thought they were a bit 'sus', but of Lionel's departure, he knew nothing.

In the general store, the owner's wife admitted that she had always considered Lionel a very dubious character, who probably had a secret family tucked away somewhere. The estate agent was able to offer her no properties for her fictitious friend, but was able to confirm that The Retreat had not been put on the market, and its owner not known to have left the area.

The hairdresser was too busy to talk, so Stella just made an appointment for the following week, then went into the tiny post office to purchase some stamps, where she, unexpectedly, hit pay dirt. The old lady who had run this establishment for what seemed like the better part of the last hundred years, told her that Lionel's mother had died some fifteen years ago.

This she knew for certain because when he had gone off to arrange the funeral and clear her house, he had his mail re-directed to her address. He had been gone three weeks, before returning with a van full of mementoes, and an even quieter disposition.

The bakery and greengrocer's yielded nothing of interest, but the butcher had a tale to tell, and he was a real old woman where gossip was concerned. Above his shop lived that legendary character, the butcher's dog, and his master took him for a long ramble through the surrounding countryside every day, after he shut up shop, weather permitting.

On two occasions, over the last couple of weeks, he had come across Lionel, out in the fields on his own, with no dog, as he didn't possess such a thing, nor reason to be there. It was unlike the man to go walking through the fields, being very much a home body, but the butcher had been interested to note that there was a strong scent of perfume coming from his clothes on both occasions, and he suspected that old Lionel was seeing someone at last, even if it was in secret.

He had continued to walk the dog towards an old tumbledown hut at the edge of the field and, there again, there was the haunting memory of perfume. The chap had been keeping trysts with someone hereabouts, and he'd give a good leg of lamb to know who it was.

This was getting more interesting as she went on. Lionel couldn't have been called away to look after his mother, simply because his mother was dead, and he'd been out and about in the fields keeping trysts with an unknown woman. There seemed to be a lot about the quiet and unassuming man that no one really knew about, and yet he didn't seem the sort to have a secret life. But then, whoever did?

Stella's last port of call was the tearooms, where she ordered a pot of tea for one and a poached egg on toast, as it was already getting on for lunchtime, and it would save her having to get something when she got home.

Just as she was tucking in, a shadow crossed her table, and she became aware of Heidi Schmidt looming over her. 'Do you mind if I join you?' she asked. 'I feel in need of confiding in someone, for I don't know what to do.'

'Help yourself,' said Stella, chewing vigorously on a mouthful of toast. 'If there's anything I can do, just fire away.'

'It is something Ferdie told me,' she began, then broke off to order a cup of coffee and a toasted tea-cake. 'He has remembered something from the night he was hit over the head, but he doesn't want to cause a fuss. He thinks it would make him unpopular.'

'What has he remembered? Something about who did it?'

'That is correct, *ja*. But he does not know what to do about what it is he is remembering.'

'Why don't you tell me what he remembered, and I'll see if I can advise you. If you decide it's best not to say anything, I'll just forget what you told me. How does that sound?'

'That sounds very sensible. He says he didn't see who hit him, for they hit him from behind, but the person said something, and he recognised the voice.'

'What did his attacker say?' asked Stella, now speaking in a whisper, as was her companion.

'He said, "That's for my daddy, you filthy Kraut." At that, Heidi's features crumpled, and she fought not to let the tears run down her cheeks.

'And whose voice was it, my dear?' asked Stella, gently, putting her hand over the shaking fingers of the German woman's.

'It was that American man's; the one they call Duke.'

'Oh, my dear, I'm so sorry. Some people seem to relish keeping hatred alive, instead of letting it die with those who were involved in it. Would you like me to get my husband to talk to the inspector about it?'

'Ferdie does not want there to be any charges. He does not want to remind people of such an appalling event in our history.'

'Don't you worry about that. I'll get Philip to speak to Inspector Falconer, and he'll see that a warning is given, but nothing is made public. Tell Ferdie everything will be sorted out with the least fuss and the greatest discretion.'

Chapter Eleven

Falconer, feeling rather more chipper after a long, hot shower and a fresh set of clothes, finally arrived at the station about eleven thirty. Carmichael was the soul of discretion, merely handing a DVD copy of the christening proceedings, to go with the one the inspector already had of the wedding, and had never viewed, feeling that it might drag up some memories that were better suppressed.

Carmichael's only comment on the ceremony the previous evening was, 'Well, that's my lot, all with their passports to heaven. No hanging around in Limbo for them. They're official now.'

The sergeant then worked diligently at his desk, and only a stray guffaw sounded, as Falconer sat like an embarrassed cat, trying to regain its dignity. Had he had the ability to sit with his legs in the air and lick the base of an imaginary tail, he would have done so.

All was quiet as an hour ticked away, then the silence was abruptly shattered by the ringing of the telephone. Falconer made a frantic grab to silence the shrillness and found Doc Christmas at the other end, puffed up with news of the doings in Fallow Fold.

'You've got a new detective on your beat, old chap: gumshoe goes by the name of Stella Christmas, and she's definitely got one over on you.'

'Are you telling me you've sent your wife out on my behalf, because I'm not up to it?' Falconer felt momentarily annoyed at this trespass on his territory. 'How would you like it if I went round cutting up bodies, to see what they'd died of?' – an offer that conjured up a distressing image of the dismembered rats the cats had left as their gift to him.

'Don't get your knickers in a twist, Harry boy. It's just the result of a conversation we had at breakfast, and you know how women love to gossip. Anyway, I am now at liberty to let you know a little something about all the hoo-ha in my home village, the first fact being that Lionel Dixon would never have left a note claiming that he'd gone to see his mother, because, apparently, his mother died fifteen years ago.'

'How on earth did you come across that little gem?'

'Stella's been out shopping on the parade, on the hunt for gossip. A woman's got a nose for that sort of thing that simply eludes us men. She also found out that our Mr Dixon has been involved in secret trysts with a mysterious unknown woman.'

'The little tinker! Anything else?'

'There's word abroad that the Maitlands aren't kosher. Oh, and the thug that attacked Ferdie Schmidt has been identified.'

'And she found out all of this, since breakfast?'

'Sure did. She's a fast worker, and no mistake.'

'Tell her I'll be over this afternoon to talk to her. Perhaps she can point me in the right direction for Shergar and Lord Lucan while she's at it.'

'Nothing would surprise me, Harry boy. Just give her a tinkle. I don't think she's planning on any more detective work, but you'd better just check.'

'Tell her not to get involved. She may think it's fun, but I feel there's real danger lurking somewhere in that village. There's more to come; I can feel it in my bones, and I'd hate for anything to happen to her, not least because you'd kill me if it did.'

'Give her a ring, make a date, then give her a rocket, with my blessing.' Doc Christmas ended the call with a smile in his voice.

Calling Carmichael abruptly to heel, like a dog that needed careful watching, they made their way downstairs to the ground floor of the station, only for Falconer to stop dead on the bottom step, causing Carmichael to bump into him. 'Pay attention, Sergeant. You nearly had me over there!'

'I didn't know you were going to stop. It's not as if you have brake-lights, you know. Anyway, why have you stopped?'

'Shh! I've just seen Dr Dubois.' Hortense Dubois, known as Honey, was a psychiatric consultant for the police, and Falconer had fallen in lust with her flawless coffee-coloured skin, neat corn-rows of hair, and her hypnotic, amber eyes. This was an opportunity to 'accidentally' bump into her that was irresistible.

'You slip out the back way. I'm just going to glide up to the front desk and engage her in casual conversation.'

Carmichael disappeared, sighing at Falconer's shyness and inability to take the bull by the horns, and just sweep her off her feet; but knowing the inspector, he'd have to take an inventory of the whole broom cupboard before he could even choose the right broom.

Falconer was more concerned, with his target now in view, with making a good impression, as he ran a hand over his hair and buffed the toes of his shoes on the back of his trouser legs. He then sauntered, in a mock-nonchalant fashion, in her direction and hailed her as if he had only just espied her.

'Good day to you, Dr Dubois. What brings you to this uncivilised neck of the woods?'

'Oh, Harry, it's you. Now, didn't I tell you to call me Honey? How are you?'

'I'm fine, if busy, so no change there then,' As he answered, he noticed that she looked rather down in the mouth, and that her eyes were tired. 'How have you been?'

'So-so. Life can't be all beer and skittles, can it?'

'You look as if life's not been terribly good to *you* lately,' Falconer stated, with more honesty than tact.

'I *am* a little down. I could do with a friend to talk things through with.'

'One friend, reporting for duty, and ready for action. How do you fancy a bite to eat in that little Italian round the back of the station? I've got to go out and conduct some interviews this afternoon, but I could meet you there about half past six?' He was chancing his arm, but maybe it would be worth it.

'Actually, I'd love to. I'll see you there, but make it seven. I've got a meeting that won't finish till after six, and I'd like to get out of my work clothes first.' Now, there was an image to conjure with! Falconer wiped the scene from his mind, and replied,

'It's a date, then.'

As she turned her attention back to the reception desk, Falconer left the building, then proceeded to skip all the way through the car park to where he had left his Boxster that morning, drawing a look of frank disbelief from Carmichael.

'Did you just win the lottery, sir?' asked the sergeant.

'Yes; in a way I did. Guess who's got a date with Dr Honey Dubois this evening?'

'No!'

'Yes! Fortune favours the brave,' replied Falconer with an ear-to-ear grin, with not a thought given to her less-than-cheerful mood.

Then his brow creased in disapproval as he stared at Carmichael's face in disbelief. 'Have you had that filthy thing through your nose all day?' he asked, wrinkling his own nose in disgust. Carmichael seemed to have acquired a nose-ring, and this, after discussing the possibility of having a tattoo.

'And what if I have?' Carmichael replied belligerently. 'After all, it's my nose, and none of your business what I do to my own body.'

'And what sort of impression is that going to make on members of the public with whom you come into contact?' Falconer was really furious with his partner.

Carmichael appeared to cough into his hand, after which he revealed his nose to be ring-free. 'Wind-up, sir; just a wind-up. I borrowed it from Kerry just to see how you'd react to it.'

'Tell Kerry that I nearly had a coronary, to think that you'd be parading yourself in public with that abomination adorning your face. I shall be having words with her. She's evidently worked out how gullible I can be,' he retorted, his face suddenly breaking out into a smile as he remembered what awaited him that evening.

In Fallow Fold, a quick visit to Stella Christmas confirmed what had already been disclosed, with a lightning verbal trip round the shops that had constituted her morning's activities. The fact that she had been so successful in her newsgathering was no skin off the inspector's nose, as it enhanced his understanding of the people he was interested in, and meant that he could get on with finding out what the hell was going on in this pretty little place.

Moving on to Rose Tree Cottage, they found Ferdie Schmidt in subdued mood, with a dressing still on the back of his head, to cover his stitches, and after the preliminary niceties, he announced in a doleful voice, 'I know who it was who hit me.'

'Has your memory returned, sir?' asked Falconer, as Ferdie had had no memory of what had happened to him from going outside for his lone vigil, to waking up in hospital.

'I remember the voice, and what it said. I never saw who did it, but what I heard has come back to me, and it makes me sad.'

'What did it say, Herr Schmidt?' Falconer was nothing

if not punctilious in his mode of address.

'It was a racist remark which I don't understand. Do I have to repeat it?'

'If you wouldn't mind, sir.'

'He said, "That's for my daddy, you filthy Kraut!" I do not even know this man's father. Why should he single me out for a punishment for something I have not done?'

Falconer cringed inwardly at the racist hatred in the remark, then asked, 'Whose voice was it, sir?'

'That American man they call Duke, although he does not appear to be very aristocratic to my eyes.'

'Do you want to press charges, sir?'

'I don't want to cause any trouble here. I will not press charges, but I think Heidi and I will look for another home. I cannot feel comfortable when there are feelings like that about.'

Carmichael sighed as he made a note of this. He found any sort of bigotry incomprehensible. We were all the same under the skin, and religion, colour, or nationality made no difference to that. That an American could act in such a foolhardy way towards a person who had not been born when the last war ended shocked him, and he felt anger growing inside him.

'Thank you for your generosity of spirit, Herr Schmidt. I'll see what I can do about scaring the living daylights out of him, with a caution down at the station, and at least you've helped us to solve one of the little mysteries that are occurring in this village. We'll have a word with him about wanton vandalism as well.'

'And don't move away because of that ignoramus, Mr Schmidt. You're settled here and part of the community. Don't let his ignorance and prejudice drive you away.' Carmichael felt he had to add something. These two, from their previous questioning, belonged to the village more than one surly American who joined in nothing. Let him move, if anyone was going to.

When Madison Zuckerman opened the door to Falconer and Carmichael's summons, her face drained of colour when she recognised they were plain-clothes policemen. 'Come in,' she hissed, 'before anyone sees you,' and she grabbed them, each by an arm, and pulled them through the doorway.

'I know why you're here. Duke told me.' Her husband had finally confessed to what he had done, when her anxiety grew to a level that even he could not ignore, and his growing sense of guilt had done the rest. 'Well, you won't find him. He's flown back to the States and, if necessary, he'll have to stay there as a fugitive, rather than come back here and face arrest, and perhaps even prison.'

'Don't be so melodramatic, Mrs Zuckerman. This is Britain, not the United States. We are well aware of what your husband has done, which amounts to common assault and actual bodily harm, but we've just spoken to his victim. Herr Schmidt remembers what your husband yelled before hitting him, and I must say I'm disgusted at the sentiments.

'However, the gentleman involved has, very magnanimously in my opinion, declined to press charges. When you speak to your racist husband, perhaps you could tell him that his victim is a great deal more civilised in his approach to the matter, and does not wish to seek revenge via the process of law.'

That was it for Madison, and she broke down into sobs, subsiding into a large deep-cushioned sofa with her head in her hands. 'His daddy was involved in the D-Day landings, and he was badly injured. In the end, he lost a leg, and was never able to work again at his old job, which was as a builder,' she explained through her weeping.

'He had to take whatever he could, working on factory lines and stuff like that. He was no intellectual, and could never have done office work. From then onwards, he was a very bitter man, and he passed that bitterness on to his son.

Duke was indoctrinated from a very early age. It was like it was bred in the bone with him.

'All I can do is apologise with all my heart. As for Duke, he's gonna have to decide whether he's coming back, now I can tell him he won't be arrested at the airport. I hope he'll seek some psychiatric help before he returns, and tries to come to terms that it was his father who was injured by someone he never knew.

'You can't direct your hatred against someone who wasn't even born when something dreadful happened. Those were other people, and other times, and we need to live in the here and now, and try to be better people than those who went before us.

'I didn't realise he still felt that strongly about it, but it must be defused. You leave it with me, and I'll let him know, in no uncertain terms, why what he did was unforgivable. I mean, how would he feel if a person of Vietnamese or Korean origin suddenly attacked him just because he was American? Duke never served in the army. He has flat feet. Oh, I'm beginning to ramble. Please forgive me, but the strain of the last few days has taken its toll.'

'You tell Duke that he can come back, but that one of my superior officers will be issuing him with a police caution. If he steps out of line again, he won't be treated so lightly, and it's only due to the generous decision of Herr Schmidt that he won't be appearing in court on a very serious charge. Ring me when he returns.'

Back in the car, Carmichael looked at Falconer with a new respect. 'Blimey, sir!' he exclaimed. 'You had me feeling guilty and worried for a moment, there. That wasn't 'alf bad! Firm, but fair.'

'I only hope Duke doesn't come looking for me when he gets back.'

'Why's that, sir?'

'He's *huge*! I wouldn't stand a chance!'

When Falconer returned home, he was pleased to note that his home appeared to be, at last, cat proof, and he sang in the shower at the sheer joy of enjoying Honey's company for a whole evening. He had it all planned out.

First, he'd entertain her with some little anecdotes about the more bizarre and amusing incidents that he had experienced in his time in the force, maybe he'd even cover her hand with his on the table.

Then he'd take her home for coffee, put on some seductive music in the background, and see if he couldn't live up to the mood of the music. Tonight would be a landmark in his life, if all went according to plan, and who knew what it might lead to?

He dressed with extraordinary care, ensuring that everything he wore, right down to cufflinks and tiepin, were coordinated. He had splashed a citrus-based cologne on after his shower and felt that he looked, and smelled, the best that he could for their rendezvous.

He had no trouble finding a parking space, and put this down as a good omen for what was to come later, arriving at the restaurant door at exactly the appointed hour, to find Honey already there, ensconced at a corner table, away from the hurly-burly of the window tables.

As he approached, his mind was taken up with running through his Italian pronunciation, so that he should make a good job of ordering for them, and he didn't notice that she wore a worried frown, and was merely dressed in clean jeans and a white T-shirt, seeming preoccupied with her own thoughts.

'Good evening, Honey,' he greeted her, and was surprised to find her reaction to his arrival slow.

'Oh, hello there. I didn't notice you come in. I was lost in my own thoughts, but now you're here, I'm sure you can make me feel better.'

A woman would have noticed an alarm bell ringing in, not only what she said, but the way in which she said it, but Falconer was male, and his antennae were not sensitive enough for such subtleties. 'Have you ordered a drink, yet?' he asked brightly.

'No, I thought I'd wait for you. I'll have a large red wine.'

Calling for a waiter, her date ordered her drink and a glass of mineral water for himself, and obtained copies of the menu.

She was very quiet throughout the first course, and it was only when she was on her second glass of red wine that she was bold enough to ask if she could come back to his for coffee afterwards. He, of course, agreed with alacrity, but something wasn't right. Her eyes were sad and she looked, somehow, forlorn in a way that tugged at his heart-strings.

'There's something bothering you, isn't there?' he asked, finally tuning-in to her mood.

'You're right about that, and I need someone to talk to that I can trust.'

'Go ahead. You know you can tell me anything,' announced Falconer, with no idea how wrong he could be.

She sat in silence for a while, while the main course was served, crumbling a piece of bread on to her napkin, and it was only then, that he noticed she had hardly touched her first course.

'Come on,' he coaxed her. 'A problem shared is a problem halved.'

'Look, I won't beat about the bush,' she started, as if she had suddenly made the decision to get this over with, whatever 'this' was.

'I went back to the Caribbean for the New Year to see family I hadn't seen in a long time. I had some leave due, and I fancied a bit of winter sunshine to cheer me up.'

'Quite natural, I would have thought,' commented Falconer, but was immediately silenced as Honey held up a hand. 'I need to tell this without interruption, because it's not something I'm proud of, and I'm finding it very difficult.'

'Sorry. I'll keep quiet until you've finished.'

'While I was out there, I, sort of, met someone. He was a friend of the family, he made me laugh, and I hung around with him a lot.'

Falconer's face had fallen, and he felt like he had a large stone in the pit of his stomach. Something told him he was going to learn something about which he'd rather know nothing.

'Anyway, one thing led, inevitably, to another,' she continued, looking down at her fingers, which were still crumbling bread, her main course sitting untouched, to one side of the table. 'It was just a bit of a laugh at the time; some silly holiday romance that was just a short-term fling, and that was it.

'Except that it wasn't. In February, I realised I was pregnant, and I had no idea what to do about it. I couldn't tell the father. He'd just be furious with me for missing some of my pills. I couldn't tell my parents, because they'd die of shame. I also didn't want to be lumbered with a baby when my career was going so well, but I had my religious upbringing to fight against.

'In the end, I took the logical, what I thought was sensible, decision, and had an abortion. It was the hardest decision I ever had to make, and now I just feel empty all the time, as if there's a vital part of my body that's simply not there any more, and I wonder if my decision was wrong.'

Falconer felt as if he had been drenched in ice-water. He felt as if his heart would break in two, such is the shock of watching someone one adored from afar, fall from their pedestal upon which you'd placed them, and prove to have feet of clay. What she said had distorted time so much for him, that he felt that worlds had ended and others begun, since she started speaking. Certainly, his own private world would never be the same again. He couldn't just sit here in silence, though: he had to say something.

'I don't think I'm really hungry. Shall I get the bill?' was what came out of his mouth, although he had made no conscious plan to bring the meal to an end so early in the proceedings.

'I think that would be a good idea, then we can go back to your place for that coffee you promised me.'

Dear God! Was he going to have to go through that as well? After all he had learnt tonight? Well, he didn't have to let her stay long. He could always plead an early start in the morning – a pre-breakfast meeting that he couldn't get out of.

They both sat in silence during the drive back to his house in Letsby Avenue, neither knowing what to do to break the impasse. Falconer was aware that, in not bringing her car, she was signalling that she would like to spend the night with him, and although that had been his fervent hope earlier, the idea disgusted him now, after what he had learnt.

He was aware of it being the twenty-first century, but that could do nothing to undo his upbringing and his personal moral code. Honey had been soiled by what she had done – not so much the abortion, although he strongly disapproved, but by her lax morals.

Did she always act like a loose woman when she went back to the Caribbean? How many affairs had she had on the island? Was this normal practice for her when back there, this slackening of a moral code, to which she admitted her parents strongly adhered?

Once inside the house, he saw her settled on the sofa, before going into the kitchen to boil water for coffee. He'd make instant; he didn't want to prolong this painful evening any longer than was absolutely necessary, and just wished himself in bed with a hot drink, reading, oblivious to the real world, with all its faults and failings.

He had no sooner laid out cups and saucers on a tray when there was a piercing shriek from the living room, and he arrived in the doorway just in time to see Honey literally throw Monkey across the room. 'What, in the name of God, do you think you're doing?' he shouted, above the still shrill yells.

'It's a filthy cat! Get it away from me! Get it out!'

Falconer ran to Monkey and picked her up, snuggling her to him, as he checked her out for any injuries, and she nuzzled his face lovingly and began her exotic double purr. Two more furry bodies slunk down the stairs, and two more, from behind an armchair, strolled out to see what all the fuss was about, and Honey recommenced shrieking, and jumped on to the sofa to get away from them.

'Get rid of them!' she yelled, and found Falconer yelling back at her.

'How dare you treat an animal like that! They are my *family*. *They* live here, and I *love* them. How dare you lay a finger on any one of them!'

'Well, shut them up somewhere,' she shouted. The two large glasses of red wine that she had consumed in the restaurant on an empty stomach must have begun to affect her, for she suddenly changed her mood and almost crooned at him.

'Throw the nasty cats out and let's go upstairs. You know that's what you want to do. You've wanted to for ages, and I could do with a little bit of comfort myself.' Then she screeched again, as Meep leapt up on the sofa and began to wind herself, as best she could on the uncertain surface, round her ankles.

'Get off me! Get off me!'

Falconer gently laid Monkey down and removed Meep from Honey's feet, fearful that she would kick the unsuspecting animal. Never before in his life had he had such an urge to strike a woman, as he did now, and he realised he had also suffered from what he could only describe as a rush of parental feeling for his charges, as if they were his children, 'I think you'd better leave, don't you?'

'How can you prefer these creatures to me?' she spat out in anger. 'You could easily get rid of them, and I could move in. We'd make a great team.'

'Because these "creatures", as you call them, only ever kill for food, and not because it may affect their career, or their social standing.' There! He's said the unthinkable!

'You pathetic little man!' she howled. 'How dare you judge me? How dare you even think you could have me? I'll see myself out and call a taxi from my mobile.'

Stalemate.

'Well, go on, then. Go!'

'I can't.'

'Why not?'

'I can't get down until you shut those cats in the kitchen, so I can get to the front door.'

'You'll have a long wait, then,' Falconer replied, suddenly rebelling at everything the evening had dealt him, and he picked up a newspaper and settled himself into an armchair to read it.

How could he ever have thought that she was beautiful? She looked anything but, with her face screwed up into a bad-tempered mask, a snarl marring what he had previously thought of as the perfection of her lips. She looked ugly and full of hatred, and he felt he had had a glimpse into her soul, and he had not liked what he had seen.

It would be a long time before he would be able to bring himself to be anything other than coldly civil towards her, and it struck him that he had just witnessed another attack borne simply out of blind prejudice. He'd rather live the rest of his life alone with his pets, than get tangled up with someone like that.

Finally the scales had fallen from his eyes: his goddess was a mere mortal, and one that despised felines and had little regard for human life. He could no more consider a future with her than he could with anyone with such character traits.

He went to bed that night, a sadder but wiser man.

Chapter Twelve

Friday

The next morning, he came down to find Monkey growling at something that seemed to be hidden behind a cushion on the sofas and, on investigation, it proved to be Honey's silk scarf from her disastrous visit the previous evening. Placing it in a plastic carrier bag, he determined to give it to Bob Bryant behind the desk, for the thought of handing it back personally was unthinkable.

'There you go. All gone, now,' he reassured the little brown cat and, intelligent as she was, she limped, holding a forepaw in the air until he left for work. It made him smile for the first time that day, as he had seen her land fairly and squarely on all four paws, and had checked her over himself to reassure himself that there was no injury. She was going to milk this one for all it was worth, if her behaviour before, during, and after breakfast was anything to go by.

Although he hadn't slept well, Falconer did his best to act as if nothing abnormal had happened the night before, and he received two phone calls shortly after his arrival in the office that both required visits, and helped to keep him distracted.

The first was from Wanda Warwick of Shepford St Bernard, enquiring if there had been any sightings of Bonnie Fletcher, who had been missing from her home for some time now. There had been appeals on local television and radio, and several sightings had been phoned in, but most were anonymous, and all those followed up, proved to be fruitless.

Unless the young woman had decided to do a disappearing act, it must be assumed that some sort of accident, or worse, had befallen her for, as he said to Wanda, if she was alive and didn't want to be found, she wouldn't be. She could easily have changed her hair colour, her style of dress, and her make-up, and then no one would know her at a casual glance, probably not even her own parents.

These last he agreed to visit again, just in case there had been something to alert them to her whereabouts, and this he did on his own, before he had even had a morning coffee. He needed something to take his mind off the terrible happenings yesterday evening, and this seemed like just the ticket.

Carmichael was seated in his usual place when he returned, just in time to receive a call from Mabel Wickers in Fallow Fold, with a request that they come out to see her, as she had some information that might prove useful to them in their investigations.

This second distraction, appearing so close to the first one, was to be welcomed, and he alerted Carmichael, even suggesting that they really ought to pop into the hospital and see how Roberts was doing, as they had been neglecting him of late. This would eat a little more of the day and stop him from brooding.

Mabel had been watching for the car, and as she opened the door to them, he could hear her old-fashioned kettle whistling away on the gas hob. After presenting them with a laden tray, a plate of home-made sponge cake taking star position in the centre, she pinned Falconer with a gimlet eye, and said, 'I have a confession to make.'

'Don't tell me it was you that went out on a vandalism spree,' he joked with her, and Carmichael choked on the mouthful of cake he had been masticating.

'You tease. Of course it wasn't, but I believe you received an unsigned letter recently, alluding to the perpetrator of the distressing goings-on in this village.'

'Perfectly correct, madam. It indicated that the anonymous writer knew who had been up to no good, which is more than I do, at the moment. Do you happen to know who it was that sent the letter in question?'

'Don't rag me. You know damned well it was me, or I wouldn't have called you. I've been away, spending some time with a friend, but I spent most of it regretting my precipitate action in putting that little fire-cracker in the post-box, so I thought I'd better get myself off home and make a clean breast of it.'

'So it was you?'

'Of course it was, but I wouldn't have sent it if I hadn't had good reason.'

'We're all ears, especially Carmichael. Ears like a bat, he's got. That's why he often wears a hat.' He was babbling, and he knew it.

Carmichael looked up at that point, just as he was helping himself to a third slice of cake.

'See what I mean?' Mabel laughed, and Carmichael frowned. Had he missed something?

'I wrote it because I had a visit from Lionel Dixon, the chap from The Retreat who runs the Bridge Circle.' She paused, before continuing, 'I don't know how much you know.'

'Let's pretend we know nothing, then you won't miss anything by assuming we already know it,' Falconer advised her.

'Fair deal. Bridge Circle is on a Monday evening, and Lionel always hosts it, providing plates of tasty little mouthfuls and drinks, and everyone makes a contribution towards his costs. He's only ever cancelled one meeting before, when he had influenza a couple of years back.

'On that occasion, he was punctilious about phoning every member with his apologies, so that no one would turn out on a cold evening to find that the meeting had been cancelled, because he didn't want to pass on what he had to anyone else.

'This Monday just past seemed the same as any other Monday, but when we arrived, there was no answer to either the bell or the knocker. Anyway, to cut a long story short, Lionel wasn't there, there were no lights on, and just a note on the mantelpiece to say he'd been called to his mother's bedside, or some other rot. His mother's been dead for fifteen years; that I do know.

'He'd come to visit me, however, the day before, after church, to get a few things off his chest. He seemed to have a bee in his bonnet about the Maitlands, who are his next door neighbours, hinting at all sort of underhand doings on their part, or at least on his – Melvyn's, that is.'

'Like what?' Falconer interrupted her flow, as it seemed the details were a necessary part of the tale.

'He seemed to think that he was working on the black, and avoiding any tax and national insurance that he could – keeping under the radar, I suppose you'd call it. Anyway, he was very agitated about it, although I didn't understand him to have a personal grievance against them. He sort of hinted, though, that a lot of the things that happened could be traced back to Melvyn Maitland.

'Now, true or not, he seemed absolutely convinced of the man's guilt. I pondered on that one for a while, and thought I'd get it off my chest by sending that stupid letter. So here I am, my hands up, wondering what you're going to do about me.'

'Absolutely nothing, madam. What we will do, is try to speak to both Mr Dixon and Mr Maitland, either to gather some evidence, or to identify whether there's some personal grudge between them. By the way, this is delicious cake. Did you make it yourself? Isn't it lovely, Carmichael?'

He knew full well that Carmichael's mouth was absolutely stuffed, and stifled a private chortle as his sergeant sprayed the carpet with crumbs trying to reply.

'I made it first thing. Would you like the last piece, Sergeant?' she asked politely, discreetly sweeping Carmichael's unexpected gift of crumbs from the lap of her skirt with one of her broad hands.

'He might as well. He's eaten most of the rest of it,' murmured Falconer, a curious numbness pervading his body and soul. He must be in a state of mild shock over Honey suddenly showing her true colours.

On their way over to see if they could raise any answer at either The Retreat or Black Beams, Carmichael asked him if there was anything wrong, having noticed a difference in his behaviour, and being concerned about it.

'Wrong, Sergeant? What could possibly be wrong? Apart from the fact that Dr Dubois is a spread-legged whore.'

'You what, sir?' Carmichael had stopped dead in his tracks, doubting either his hearing or his sanity. 'What did you say?' He was so taken aback to hear Falconer refer to anyone in such strong language that he hardly knew how to react. 'That's a bit harsh, isn't it, sir? I thought you thought she was the bee's knees.'

'Well, I was wrong, OK? And I don't want to discuss it any more. Got it, *Sergeant*?'

'Sorry I spoke.' Carmichael felt quite offended to be so treated and definitely rebuffed.

'Oh, just ignore me. I'm in a deep sulk, and I don't feel up to discussing it at the moment. You can rest assured, though, that when I do need to talk, you'll be the first person I turn to, because I know I can trust your discretion.'

'Look, sir, if you ever need company, someone to talk to, or simply somewhere else to be, you're always welcome at our house. If you're hungry, we'll gladly feed you. If you're tired, we'll always have a bed for you. And if you just want to sit up all night talking, I'll keep you company, and so will Kerry. Between us, we could talk the proverbial hind legs off a donkey, and neither of us are gossips. Don't be a stranger, OK, sir?'

'Thank you very much, Carmichael. That means a lot to me,' Falconer replied gravely, then lapsed, once more into silence. He had suddenly realised how lonely he had been feeling, and this was probably due to the aloofness he radiated, not because he didn't want to be sociable, but because, although no one would believe it, he was, underneath all the things he had to be to do his job efficiently, a shy person, who found it very difficult to be 'one of the crowd'. He found it impossible to show his feelings in the way others seemed to do, without having to think about it.

Back in business mode once more, they worked their way round The Retreat first, finding the back door still unsecured. On entering, everything seemed to be in order, and Falconer sent Carmichael upstairs ahead of him, while he took a quick scout around the ground floor.

It was no longer than two minutes later when he heard a scream which wouldn't have disgraced a virgin about to be deflowered against her will, and he headed up the staircase, two steps at a time, to see what had produced this alarming reaction from his sergeant. Maybe he had found Mr Dixon, horribly dead, somewhere up there.

What he discovered was Carmichael, standing in the bathroom, squealing with horror and disgust, and pointing at the bath. 'It's in there, sir, and it's an absolute monster,' he explained. Having no idea what to expect, Falconer took a look to reveal the presence of only a lone spider, albeit a very large and hairy specimen. 'It's only a spider, Carmichael. What's all the fuss about?'

'Get rid of it, sir. Get rid of it *now*! I can't abide the things, and neither can Ma.'

'How did she cope when you were little?'

'She got Dad to deal with them.'

'And now?'

'Kerry actually picks them up,' here he shuddered from head to toe, 'and puts them outside. And if she's not around, one of the boys does it. She's brought them up not to be afraid of them, because they're so much smaller than them. *Get rid of it* before I pass out.'

Falconer was not very fond of the eight-legged horrors either, but boldly turned on a tap, flushed it down the plug-hole, then inserted the plug to prevent its return by the same route. If any appeared in his own house, he used to have an unwritten agreement with Mycroft, that they were his, to do with what he wished. Now there were five spider-prevention units in the house, to cover his own disgust at the creatures, and his rather cowardly attitude towards their presence.

'There you go, Carmichael,' he stated. 'All gone!' then had to put his hands in his pockets, to hide the fact that they were trembling, if only very slightly. Never had he proved so heroic before about dealing with one of these particular horrors.

What would they say at the station if they knew he had almost a strong a horror of arachnids as did his sergeant? He'd be a laughing stock, and, no doubt, the butt of several practical jokes involving fake or real eight-legged fiends, probably with Merv Green as the ring-leader.

Present danger overcome, they began to search the first floor together – there might be more of them up here, as the house had been standing empty, and he'd rather come face-to-maw with them with Carmichael than without him.

Everything looked fine until they got to the main bedroom, where the contents of drawers and cupboards were spilled everywhere in confusion, as if someone had been frantically searching for something they couldn't find.

Clothes covered the floor and the dressing table that must once have belonged to Lionel's mother, shoes were scattered around, and even the mattress sat askew, as if someone had been looking underneath it for whatever they sought. The whole room looked like it had been hit by a whirlwind.

Downstairs once more, Carmichael riffled through the post that had accumulated in the hall, but there was nothing of interest there, apart from the usual junk mail and bills. Downstairs, pot plants were wilting, and a bunch of flowers in a vase in the middle of the dining table drooped its stems in pathetic arcs, its blooms bow-headed towards the table top, sitting as it did now in brown water.

Suddenly attracted by the 1930s clock garniture on the mantelpiece, Falconer wandered over to it, and found there was a letter tucked behind it. Maybe this was another one abut visiting his dead mother, he thought facetiously. But it wasn't, and he read: *I think Mel knows about us. Be very careful. M xxx*

'Carmichael!' he called. 'Come and look at this.' When the sergeant had read the short missive, Falconer asked him what he thought it meant.

'It looks to me as if Mr Dixon was having a clandestine relationship with Mrs Maitland,' he speculated.

'Yes,' agreed Falconer with a sour smile. 'Another faithless bitch in a world without hope.'

'I say, sir! That's a bit strong, isn't it?'

'Not from my point of view. Hello, what's this on the hearth tiles? Looks a bit like blood to me.' On the base of the fireplace there was a smear of something brown that looked as if it had started out as red.

'Take a sample of that, Sergeant, and get it straight to the forensic lab as soon as we get back. I'll grab a hairbrush I saw in the bedroom for them to get comparison DNA. We need to know whether this is his blood or someone else's.

'Our Mr Dixon's been gone for some time, though,' Falconer declared. 'I think we're going to have to visit some of the neighbours, to see when he was last seen. If nobody's seen him since before last Monday, we'll probably have to report him as a missing person. They seem to be all the rage at the moment,' he commented, thinking of Bonnie Fletcher. 'Let's try Black Beams, see what the Maitlands have to say.'

'Doesn't seem to be a lot of life in there, either,' commented Carmichael, focusing on curtains half-drawn and windows all shut up tight on such a lovely day.

But they could raise no answer there, either, and there were no conveniently unlocked doors to this house to grant them ingress. The curtains in the kitchen and what they presumed to be a utility room were fully drawn, and they were thick enough to obscure any details of the interior.

'We'll have to leave it for now. Perhaps we can get a search warrant, which will allow us to gain entry. There's not much point in doing that till after the weekend, and they might just come back, and the problem will be solved.'

On the drive back, Falconer once more lapsed into an introspective silence, the only comment that passed his lips, being when they arrived back at the station and, just when they were about to get out of the car, he said, 'The trouble with me, Carmichael, is that I can only do black and white. I'm simply no good at shades of grey,' apropos of nothing that Carmichael could identify. 'Oh, and don't forget to hand in that blood sample and hairbrush, and tell them I want the result yesterday.'

Carmichael kept his lip buttoned. The inspector would talk when he was ready. He could wait till then, when the man had decided whether or not he wanted to share whatever had knocked the stuffing out of him and left him subtly altered.

The DS dealt with the process of reporting Lionel

Dixon missing, submitting a photograph he had half-inched when they went through the house. They'd only have had to go back for one, if he hadn't managed to acquire this one on the sly, and Falconer didn't seem at the top of his game at the moment.

In the B&B in Carsfold, the couple who had registered to stay for a night or two announced their intention of leaving in the morning, as their car would be ready, then retired to their room to discuss plans that needed to be carried out before the next day.

'We ought to have all three with us,' one of them said. 'It's always handy to have a spare.'

'But where are they?' the other replied, 'And we've still got that other little job to finish off. We can't leave that undone, or it'll be *our* undoing. Did you bring the letters?'

'Shit, no! I completely forgot about them. We'll go back later and get the job finished. That's got to be done before dark. Then I think we'd better come back here and make sure we've got everything planned as it should be,' said the first.

'We'll go back again in the early hours and do the searching. That won't require much light, and I doubt if anyone would notice a torch in the middle of the night. And there's something else I must pick up that I forgot before, but I'll do that on the first visit.'

Before the two detectives had got settled at their desks, Carmichael gave a hoot of despair, and said, 'We forgot to visit Roberts!'

'What a pair of callous bastards we are,' replied Falconer, hardly lifting his head from the paperwork that lay on the desk in front of him.

'Oh, come on, sir. Don't take out whatever's eating you on him. He's had a really nasty experience, and I don't

146

think he's made a lot of friends locally, yet. He'll probably be really glad to see us.'

Falconer sighed a sigh of the terminally weary, and dragged himself into an upright position. 'All right, St Francis, let's go and get some grapes and flowers, and go listen to him describe his operation in minute detail. I can't think of anything better to do, and at least it'll pass the time.'

As the day wore on, the sun disappeared behind the heavy dark clouds that threatened a storm to come, before the day was out, and within an hour, large drops of rain began to fall, turning the scene from the office window from one of almost continental brightness to one of grey tarmac, drab mackintoshes and a sea of umbrellas, all viewed through the obscuring curtain of heavy rain.

No one was strolling now, but became just figures hidden under large circular protectors, scurrying about their business so as to spend as little time as possible outside. The wind was getting up, too, and the odd umbrella turned inside out when hit with an unexpectedly strong gust of wind.

The sky darkened much earlier than it should have done at this time of year, and the street lamps were reacting to this reduction of light by coming on early. All in all, it had turned into an absolutely filthy late afternoon, and the call from Mabel Wickers was not welcomed by either man.

'Looks like we're going out again, instead of packing up to go home. That was that Wickers woman on the phone again,' explained Falconer, who had answered the call. 'She says she has just seen a light moving about in The Retreat, as if there's someone in there with a torch. She doesn't want to go over herself, in case she gets attacked, so she's decided that we can rush over there, probably arriving much too late or, if in time, to get attacked on her behalf.'

'I don't know what's eating you, sir, but I'll be glad when it leaves off. I've never known you so hard-hearted and abrupt as you've been today. You're just not yourself.'

'Nor do I want to be, for the time being, so you'd better keep your neb out until I'm ready to spill the beans. OK, Sergeant?'

'OK, sir. If that's the way you want it to be,' replied a hurt and crestfallen Carmichael.

'And we'll take separate cars, too, so that we can just go home afterwards, without having to come back to this dump, and I won't have to listen to you drivelling on about how wonderful life is – because frankly, at the moment, it isn't, for me, even if it is for you and all the hundreds of other little Carmichaels that make up your narrow little world.'

'If you say so, sir.'

The storm was fierce when they left the station, and it took them an unprecedented half an hour to reach the village of Fallow Fold. Only cresting the femininely curvaceous hill on which it was situated revealed how exposed the place was, as the wind suddenly howled across the un-wooded land, buffeting both cars with a ferociousness that neither driver had expected. The rain up here didn't fall, but was almost horizontal, driven by such a fierce gale.

On arrival, separately and miserably, they went straight to Sideways, to see if Mabel Wickers had a further update for them. She was soaked through and drying her rats' tails hair with a towel when she opened the door to them, explaining that she had, of necessity, had to go outside a few steps down the road to get a good view of the property.

From this damp vantage point, she had kept a constant eye on the supposedly abandoned house, and was able to inform them that the light stopped flickering about ten minutes ago. She'd seen no one leave, but then she'd seen no one arrive either. Promising them a hot drink when

Chapter Thirteen

Saturday – The Early Hours

'I phoned Carmichael first,' said the voice of Bob Bryant, while Falconer was still searching for his wits. He had taken a sleeping tablet before he got into bed, so that even if he had nightmares, he would get a sound night's sleep in which to dream them.

Suddenly, he realised he was sitting bolt upright in bed with the telephone in his hand, and a voice was squawking from it, un-listened to. 'Sorry, Bob, what was that? I didn't catch it.' Good grief! The clock said three o'clock!

'I said I've sent Carmichael off to Fallow Fold. He's nearest, so I rang him first, but I want you to get over there a well. Some old dear's reported at least two people, or at least two torches, in a house that's been unoccupied for probably a few days now. I want it checked out, even if it's a waste of time. You never know, and I know you've had some dealings over there, so there might be a connection.'

By the time Falconer had dragged his still half-drugged body out of bed, Carmichael was dressed and about to leave his house. 'I won't be long, sweetheart, and I'll take Mulligan with me, just in case I need a miscreant licked to death.'

'Well, he wouldn't be much use as a guard dog, would he? He's much too friendly. And I wouldn't recommend him as a bloodhound either. He simply hasn't got the looks for it,' Kerry Carmichael laughed up into her husband's face, then kissed him goodbye.

'See you for breakfast,' she said, and waved him out of

the house. He was somewhat delayed in his departure as Mulligan had decided he didn't want to sit in the back seat, and suddenly became a canine eel who slipped out of Carmichael's grasp every time he thought he had the dog defeated.

The dog won, of course, as dogs tend to, and his temporary guardian compromised, with the huge animal lolling upright in the passenger seat, seatbelt sensibly about him, his full attention on the road ahead, and one huge paw on Carmichael's left leg, which he used for expressing his opinion of the man's driving.

The sergeant was unable to take the empty country roads as fast as he would have liked because the storm had not yet abated, and was still rumbling round this part of the countryside, rain still pouring from the heavens like a cataract. As he drove higher into the downs towards Fallow Fold, the wind seemed to increase its force considerably, and his vehicle was shaken from side to side with its wild buffeting, reminding him of his earlier trip there.

He really would have to get a new, or newer, car, he thought as he drove. His old Skoda had been on its last legs for a couple of years, now and, although it had proved to be reasonably reliable, his luck couldn't last forever.

It was, after all, mainly held together with rust, and when that gave out he could be left driving along with no body-work whatsoever, naked from the steering wheel up. Maybe he'd ask Falconer's advice as to what to buy, when the black mood his boss had been in today finally lifted and he returned to being his pompous old self.

After a somewhat precarious drive through the tempest, he stopped the car just short of Black Beams and parked it outside The Retreat. It was doubtful that anyone inside the house would have heard the car's engine, as the gods seemed to be practising ten-pin bowling up above, and crash after crash of thunder followed lightning as vivid as a laser show.

Undoing Mulligan's seatbelt, he told the dog to be a good boy and not to make any noise, in the simple belief that the monster canine understood every word that was said to him, and the two of them approached Black Beams, keeping to any shadow cover that they could.

As soon as they had left the shelter of the car, the wind took them, and nearly bowled both of them over. It was as wild a night as Carmichael could remember, and they could only make any forward progress by leaning into the wind and forcing their way through its onslaught.

There were no signs of life from the front of the house, so they worked their way slowly round towards the back, step by careful step. Carmichael kept hold of the dog's collar, and thus was aware of an almost silent rumbling in the animal's throat, above the shrieking of the storm, but it reached him more as a vibration, such was the racket from the wind and rain.

A slight pull on the collar halted the dog, so that Carmichael could listen. A momentary lapse in the lightning showed a weak light coming from the very back of the property, and in the few seconds' silence, he heard voices coming from the same direction, raised against the superior voice of nature. So there *was* someone here. There was no sign of the inspector yet, so he'd better take this slowly and carefully.

When he indicated that he wanted to move forward, Mulligan suddenly dug in his paws, the hackles on his neck and all down his back rising, and the growling in his throat grew a little louder and more menacing.

'What's up, Mulligan? What's making you so agitated?'

Carmichael's sense of unease grew, but he didn't falter and, letting go of the dog's collar, moved as quietly as he could towards the rear entrance of the house. Any noise he made would be covered by the sound of the few trees in the garden thrashing their branches in the wind, and the groaning they made as the onslaught hit them with every fresh gust.

Anything that wasn't fixed down became ammunition for the wind to toss at the unwary, and he could hear the sound of metal dustbins jangling on concrete paths, as the wild weather played them like a musical instrument.

Empty crisp packets, soft drink cans, wrapping papers, empty dinner-for-one microwave boxes: all hit their mark as they danced maniacally to nature's tune, but Carmichael preserved his concentration, not allowing anything to distract him from his undetected approach to whoever was in the rear of the property.

It was an act of sheer bad luck that led to his discovery. As a sheet of flapping newspaper, seeking an avian life of its own, was deposited on Mulligan's head and over his face, the dog let out a howl of fear and surprise.

There was a shout from a rear room of the house, Carmichael shot round the corner, realising that his cover was blown, then stopped dead in his tracks, unable to believe what his eyes were telling him was right in front of him. He really should have obeyed his first instinct, which was to flee.

On the floor of the utility-cum-garden room was a severed arm, amidst a lake of blood, beside it, a woman holding its twin. He opened his mouth to shout 'police', but nothing happened. He was mute with shock.

A powerful torch was suddenly shone in his eyes, and while he was still blinded, something lunged at his body, and he felt a paralysing pain across his gut and sank, still silent, to the floor, clutching at where the pain was most acute, but there seemed to be something in the way, something sticking out of him and, although he had no idea what it was, he knew he was in serious trouble.

For a second or two, a light was switched on, and the prone figure looked down at himself, to see a garden fork, apparently growing out of his middle, his lower half slowly soaking with blood that flowed now, unchecked, from his wounds.

He tried to call for help, but could still not utter a sound. Almost immediately, his vision began to fade to black and white, and the last thing of which he was aware before slipping into unconsciousness, was Mulligan, barking and growling in fury.

Across Ploughman's Lays, Stella Christmas roused her husband, to alert him to the furious barking and baying of what sounded like the hound of the Baskervilles, across the road at what was, presumably, Back Beams, for Mulligan's bark was commensurate with his frame, in volume. 'Phil, get up! There's something going on over the road,' she urged her husband.

'It's just a dog,' he mumbled, turning over and tying to slip back into the rather pleasant dream he had been enjoying.

'But there aren't any dogs over there, and this one sounds as if it's going to attack someone. At least take a look out of the window.'

Doc Christmas did as he was bidden, knowing there would be no more sleep for him that night if he didn't satisfy Stella's curiosity, although why she couldn't go to the window herself, he didn't know.

No sooner had he parted the curtains, than he began to behave like a lunatic, grabbing at items of clothing, almost tearing them in his rush to get them on. He grabbed his mobile phone from his bedside table, and told Stella to keep an eye out on what was going on across the road.

In reply to her urgent pleas for information as to why his departure now seemed so urgent, he merely replied, 'Carmichael's car is outside The Retreat and, if I'm not mistaken, that mad dog is the one he's looking after. He's in some sort of trouble over there. Phone the station and see if they can get a car out here immediately. And you! Do *not* leave the house. Just watch from up here. If I need you, I'll call. I've got my phone.'

He shot out of the house as if taking part in a hundred-yards dash, and Stella could see him haring across the road towards the source of the howling and barking.

Falconer dressed in a somewhat more leisurely way, in the mood to resent being roused from his bed on what was probably another wild goose chase. Carmichael lived nearer, and would probably get there first and, by the time he arrived, the sergeant would have whatever it was all sewn up, and the inspector would be surplus to requirements. For a few seconds, he even considered not answering the call at all, but this was against his basic nature. He just wouldn't hurry, that's all.

It was an absolutely foul night, and he'd drive as carefully as one who had just passed the driving test. Why should he endanger himself because some old biddy was imagining things? How could anyone see anything in these conditions? No he'd get there, and it would all be a false alarm over an imaginary sighting.

Such were the thoughts that ran through his self-pitying mind as he crawled through the countryside, fighting the fierce crosswinds that threatened to drive his Boxster off the road and making him realise how exposed and high Fallow Fold was, but confident that he would be back in his own bed within the hour, with absolutely nothing achieved.

Doc Christmas followed the urgent summons of Mulligan, and found himself in the middle of hell itself. The dog was keeping two blood-stained people at bay at the end of the room that boasted no door, there were two dismembered arms on the floor in a welter of blood and, lying inside this stomach-churning sea of blood was another, identifiable as

Davey Carmichael.

'Carmichael!' he cried hoarsely, noting with horror that the young man had a garden fork sticking out of his gut area and, although he was still breathing, was unconscious either from shock, loss of blood, or a combination of the two.

After a moment of indecision as to what to do first, he retrieved his mobile phone from his pocket and rang for an ambulance, then for good measure, asked for police to attend as well. He next called Stella, just said 'Blankets' to her, and knelt to attend to his gravely wounded patient.

His mind was in a torment of what to do for the best. Should he remove the fork and risk internal bleeding and seeping, which could produce septicaemia, or should he leave it in situ until paramedics arrived? He eventually decided that he'd remove the obscenity, so that he could at least pack the individual piercings to try and minimise blood loss.

He'd been a qualified doctor for years, but tonight he felt like a first year medical student again. This was, after all, someone he knew. This was someone with whom he had shared a joke, and worked. This was a young man, not long married, with a wife and three children. Eventually, his professional attitude reasserted itself, and he decided on a course of action.

As he surveyed the angle that the tines of the fork had entered the body, he began to work out the best way to ease the unlikely weapon from the young man's body. Carmichael groaned, his eyes briefly opened, only to roll back again into the welcome embrace of unconsciousness, and all the while Mulligan kept up his growling and howling at the two people cowering at the other end of the room.

Suddenly the cold wet cloth of reality hit the doctor in the face, and he realised that even to attempt such an action in his present surroundings would be foolhardy beyond belief. The fork needed to be removed in a hospital, where all the necessary staff and pieces of equipment were at hand to deal with the unexpected. In reality, the only course of action open to him was to make sure the fork did no further internal damage by steadying it until the paramedics reached their patient.

As Falconer entered Ploughman's Lays, he noticed Carmichael's dustbin of a Skoda parked outside The Retreat, and smiled sardonically. That was it, then. The sergeant would have sorted everything out, and all there would be left for him to do would be to go back home, another disturbed night under his belt. Still, he'd better, at least, check in.

As he reached to open the car door, he spotted a figure streaking across the road, and it seemed to have come from Christmas Cottage. That brought him up short. Maybe something was going on, after all. Opening the door only helped to confirm that, as he recognised the menacing baritone bark that could only belong to Mulligan, and he began to move a little faster.

As he approached Black Beams, he became aware of Stella Christmas in dressing gown and slippers, in this weather, moving as fast as she could against the wind, and approaching Black Beams with an armful of blankets. Falconer began to run, and as he ran, he became aware of a familiar siren, some distance away still, but approaching fast. What the hell had happened? And where the bloody hell was Carmichael?

He arrived in the ramshackle room at the back of the house just as the ambulance was screeching to a halt out on the road, and what he saw would be imprinted on his brain forever. Carmichael lay in a pool of blood, a garden fork protruding from his middle, Doc Christmas surveying this horribly out-of-place garden implement with a considering frown on his face.

Doc Christmas knelt in the blood beside him, studying the garden fork so improperly employed. Stella Christmas stood beside him now, clutching an armful of blankets. Also on the floor, but currently ignored, were two dismembered arms and, at the other end of the room, crouched two figures, kept at bay by a furious Mulligan.

Falconer heard someone scream, and realised it was he who had made that high-pitched noise full of anguish and fury. One of the figures at the end of the room suddenly made a run for it, taking the opportunity that the distraction of the scream had caused.

No sooner had the sound died away, than Falconer was off after the figure. He threw off his jacket to free his arms, and Doc Christmas saw his face change from one of heartbreak to that of a newly minted demon. His eyes stared out, bulging as if they could catch the miscreant on their own, his mouth hung open, exposing his teeth in a parody of a wolf's snarl, and he was away, easily catching up with the running figure, and bringing it down with a tremendous 'whump', with a rugby tackle.

As this scene of incandescent rage was being played out, Mulligan took his place beside Carmichael and commenced to howl in grief and woe, but Falconer hadn't finished with the man yet, though, and commenced kicking and punching him, with an occasional head butt, furiously screaming that he would kill him if anything happened to his sergeant. It took two paramedics and Doc Christmas to pull him off and handcuff the man. Mulligan continued to howl.

'Now stop acting up, Harry. Distracting the paramedics from dealing with their patient won't do Carmichael any good, and time is of the essence with an injury like this.'

The doctor had been holding Falconer's arms to restrain him, but the inspector suddenly threw off his hands and knelt down by Carmichael's prone body. 'Hang in there, Carmichael,' he whispered, close to the sergeant's ear. 'Kerry and the children need you. Don't leave them. Don't leave *me*.'

As he moved away from his ear, tears dripped from Falconer's face onto Carmichael's. '*Don't leave me.* Don't you dare!' he said, once more, and then noticed that the injured officer was trying to speak.

'Tell Kerry. Love them all,' he managed to croak, before returning to a place where no one could hurt him.

Falconer had sounded like a petulant child denied a treat, but had to eventually agree with Doc Christmas that, as senior officer on side, it would be dereliction of duty for him to abandon the proceedings and go off in the ambulance with his sergeant. He had other responsibilities, and had to stay at the scene to execute them.

'I'll go with him, Harry, and stay as long as I'm allowed to. Anyway, I want you to break it to Kerry. She'll take it best from you. If you like, you can take Stella with you, and she can see about the children and getting Kerry over to the hospital. But you've got to stay here, for now. There's ample evidence of another murder, and you need to see that the evidence is handled in such a way that its integrity isn't compromised.'

'You're quite right, Doc. The only change I'd like to make would be to leave speaking to Kerry until the morning. There's no point in shocking her into wakefulness at this god-awful hour, or the children. We'll know by morning how serious things are, and she can be given an informed opinion, instead of just speculation about what's happening.'

'And what if he dies in the meantime? Would you deprive her of her last chance to say goodbye?'

Falconer winced, but replied, 'Yes. Let her remember him as he was. Anyway, he's not going to die. NOT! *Do you hear me?*' He was shouting by the time he finished his answer.

'Cool it, Harry. I'm off with the ambulance now. Do your job thoroughly, and then join me at the hospital.'

Once more, Falconer had to wear his professional mask, try to ignore his own scattered emotions, and deal with the scene in which he found himself involved. As the ambulance drew away, a car with extra officers arrived, along with a SOCO team, yawning and complaining that it would have kept till the morning, and why did they always have to be disturbed in the middle of the night?

'I don't see why you should lie in the arms of Morpheus when I'm up and about,' the inspector upbraided them, real anger in his voice. 'Do like me, and just get on with your job. And no more moaning. This is what you get paid for!'

He'd kept himself well away from the couple in handcuffs and, when he was handing them over to be taken to the station, introduced them to their new guardians. 'May I give you Mr and Mrs Melvyn Maitland?' he said, only to have a chorus of denials from the handcuffed ones, who were standing to one side of him out of the light.

Turning in utter surprise at their reaction, he pulled the man into the light, only to find himself staring into the face that appeared in the photograph that he had obtained from The Retreat. 'Mr Dixon?' he squeaked, in surprise. 'Then where's Mr Maitland?'

'Oh, he's in bits about the affair,' said Marilyn Maitland, and began to giggle.

'He's completely 'armless,' quipped Dixon, and chortled heartily.

'Where's the rest of him?' barked Falconer, disgusted by their behaviour.

'Chilling out,' replied Marilyn.

'In the freezer,' sniggered Lionel.

'But why?' Falconer was dumbfounded. 'Take them away. I'll deal with them in the morning, when I've cleaned up this mess.'

Good God! What on earth had gone on here? He'd been sure that Lionel Dixon was dead, and the blood sample obtained from his house would prove it. Now Dixon had assaulted Carmichael, possibly fatally – no, he couldn't think about that at the moment – and seemed to be in cahoots with Marilyn Maitland.

Between them, he supposed, they had murdered Melvyn, cut up his body, and just been finishing the job of dismembering him and hiding the body parts in the freezer. He could leave the sealing-off of the scene, and all the photographing and clearing up, to those whose speciality it was.

His first priority at the moment, was to get over to the hospital, and he'd have to visit Kerry, whatever the outcome. Then he'd have to interview the two murdering bastards that had been caught on the premises. Then …? Then …? He couldn't think any further ahead. His brain was paralysed with shock and grief.

A voice delayed his departure. 'Hey, sir, I've found a bundle of old letters in the woman's shoulder bag. Do you want to see? They seem to be love letters between those two they've just taken away, and the postmarks are really old.'

'Put them in an evidence bag, take them back to the station, and leave them on my desk. I don't have the energy to deal with them at the moment, but they might provide the answer for all this palaver.'

Inspector Harry Falconer walked briskly down the garden path, his head held high, his shoulders back, his sheer strength of will trying to hold body and soul together. If he loosened his grip, he'd either fall to pieces or implode.

Chapter Fourteen

Saturday

When the surgeon who had assessed Carmichael in the emergency admissions room returned, hours had passed, although it felt more like days – even weeks – to Falconer, who had played out every possible outcome to the tragic situation, and most of them were bleak in the extreme.

The surgeon's face was drawn and exhausted, and his expression was serious as he approached to explain his patient's post-operative condition.

Falconer's mouth was so dry, at the lack of a smile on the approaching figure's face, that his tongue was stuck to the roof of his mouth, and he could not speak.

DS Roberts, to whom the news had filtered through via the nurses, to the general ward, had persuaded a nurse to convey him, in a wheelchair, to join Falconer and Doc Christmas in their vigil, and managed to ask, in his usual tactless way, 'Is he dead?'

'He's not that easy to kill,' replied the surgeon, finally allowing himself a slight twitch at the corners of his mouth. 'But it was touch and go in the theatre. His heart stopped at one point, and we had to resuscitate him, but it was only a short break in output, so I don't expect there to be any permanent brain damage.

'We also didn't find any previously undiagnosed or unexpected problems, so it's all in the hands of the gods, now. He's a strong young man, so I assume he has a strong constitution to help him through this ordeal. What we do need, are some emergency stocks of blood; he's an unusual group – B Rhesus negative, and we've used most of what we carry, pumping it into him, as he leaked it out.

'That's my group!' exclaimed Falconer. 'You can take some of mine, and I'll ring the station. I'm sure there'll be volunteers there willing to contribute.'

'Park yourself in that side ward when you've made your call, and tell any volunteer donors to come to the A&E reception desk, where someone will be waiting to receive them,' said the surgeon, with relief in his voice. 'We've got some more on its way, but, boy, can your colleague bleed. In fact, I've come to the conclusion that he's a right little – or not so little – bleeder.'

'After I've been bled, can we see him?' asked Falconer, having detached his tongue from its prison on his palette, and summoned up sufficient spit to be able to utter.

'Not for a while yet, I'm afraid. We'll be keeping him sedated to give his body the best chance to start the healing process. I'll have you informed as soon as it's possible for him to receive visitors. Now, if you'll excuse me, it's been a very long night for all of us, and I'm sure we could all do with some rest.

As Falconer exited the hospital after making his contribution, he caught sight of Merv Green and Bob Bryant at the reception desk, and stopped to have a word with them.

'Where the hell's Mulligan?' was his first question. 'Surely he wasn't abandoned at the scene?'

'You mean that racehorse? No he wasn't! He's in the cell next door to those two murdering bastards, with a bowl of water, a custody blanket, and a huge helping of canteen corned-beef hash. If anyone can stop those two from making a nuisance of themselves, it's that animal. He only stops growling at them when he's eating or drinking.'

'What's going to happen to him? His owners aren't back yet, and Kerry can't handle him with everything else that's happened.'

'I'm going to take him home with me for as long as

164

necessary. He's a great dog, and it'll be company for me until I can persuade Twinkle to walk up the aisle and make an honest man of me,' offered Merv generously. There probably weren't that many who would offer Mulligan temporary shelter willingly.

Roberts had been wheeled back to the ward, and Doc Christmas, as he was leaving, advised Falconer to stop blethering and go home, have a shower and a couple of cups of strong coffee, get some food in his stomach, and he'd send Stella to meet him in Castle Farthing. Kerry had to be told, and it would be better if there were a woman present.

Falconer declined his kind offer of Stella's presence, telling him that he'd get PC Starr to accompany him, thus keeping the whole thing within the force. He felt like a robot, his thoughts and actions all on automatic pilot. He was numb, both physically and emotionally, but at least he wouldn't have to tell Kerry that she was a widow – for now.

That thought brought back Carmichael's comment about the recent baptisms, and how his whole family now had their entry to heaven, and he hoped fervently that their father wouldn't be the first to present this ticket to St Peter. He'd have a long lonely wait for the rest of the family.

The inspector drove home in a state of fugue, and only began to thaw a little when the hot needles of the shower prickled his skin. Slowly, he began to fill with fury: fury at the casual way that Honey had betrayed the budding relationship they had had; fury at the fickleness of fate that had allowed Carmichael to fall prey to a silly little man who had struck out with a deadly weapon; guiltily furious at Roberts for going down with appendicitis and not being there in Carmichael's place, although he acknowledged that this last was totally unfair, and just a product of his confused mental state.

Falconer had changed his mind about PC Starr accompanying him to Jasmine Cottage, as it was his tardy arrival in Fallow Fold that was at the root of the situation. He dressed with particular care. He had a heartbreaking task ahead of him, and he owed it to Kerry to be well turned out. It wouldn't make the news any better, but it would be a mark of respect for his colleague, and the esteem in which he held his family.

His stomach was churning as he knocked on the door of Jasmine Cottage, and a sheen of sweat adorned his forehead and top lip. This was going to be one of the hardest things he had had to do in his life, even though Carmichael was still in the land of the living, for there was no guarantee that he would remain there.

'Is that you, Davey?' called Kerry's voice. 'Have you forgotten your key again?' It was only seven thirty in the morning; who else would she be expecting at such an early hour?

The smile on her face froze as she saw the inspector standing there, dressed in his best, and she instantly noticed the putty-coloured skin and the exhaustion in his eyes. 'Oh no,' she almost wailed. 'Not Davey?'

He caught her as she slumped, and helped her into the cottage, where the boys were just finishing breakfast at the dining table. Harriet, he noticed, had finished her morning meal, as evidenced by the sticky mess on the table of her highchair, and was just visible, sleeping off her food in her pram.

'Go and play upstairs, boys,' he ordered, with a stern look, and guided Kerry to the sofa, where he gently set her down. 'Mummy and I have got to have a little talk, and you'd be *so* bored. I'll give you a call when we've finished, then you can come down again. OK?'

Slightly fazed by this unconventional happening, neither boy made a murmur about being sent from the room, and mounted the stairs without a sound. Children can sense atmosphere and, at the moment, they sensed something that they'd rather not know about for now.

Fear made Kerry start to babble, and she began with, 'He's dead, isn't he? Davey's dead? What happened? What are we going to do without him? We've had him for such a short time. He was the best father in the world, you know, and I don't know how we're going to carry on, on our own. I've been separated from one husband, the boys' father, and he died, and now Davey's dead. Oh, God! Whatever are we going to do without him?'

This last question ended in a wail of despair, and Falconer took both her hands in his, and said quietly and calmly, 'Davey isn't dead, my dear, but he has been badly injured. He's in the hospital now, where they're doing everything they can for him. He's in the best hands possible, and they'll do everything that's humanly possible for him.'

'But he's going to die, isn't he? I can hear it in your voice.'

'It's in God's hands, now, but he's been operated on. They've transferred him to the ICU, and all we can do now is to wait and pray.'

'Oh, my God!' Kerry almost sighed. 'What about Ma? Has someone broken the news to her? She'll be out of her mind with worry when she finds out.'

'I understand that Merv and Twinkle are going round to see her, then Twinkle's coming here, so that you can go to the hospital. It's all been cleared with Chivers, so don't give it another thought.' This he had discovered with his brief chat at the reception desk before he left the hospital, and was glad he had some positive information to report.

'You go on upstairs and have a bath or shower or whatever, get dressed, and try not to brood on it too much. When you're ready, Twinkle should be here, and while you're getting ready, Uncle Harry will be in charge.'

It is worthy of note that in any circumstances less serious than the ones which presently prevailed, he would no more have referred to himself as Uncle Harry than he would be to ride through the streets of Market Darley stark bollock naked.

At ten thirty he left Kerry in the ICU, sitting by her husband's bed, tears streaming down her face and mumbling frantic prayers for the patient's life to a God she'd only half-believed in before this tragedy. Carmichael lay in the bed, numerous tubes coming out of his body, machines beeping their message of 'OK, for now', but there was no way he could communicate, as he was being kept under sedation to give his body time to concentrate on healing itself.

Carmichael himself was in a place of limbo. He was aware of strands of sound, which he knew were voices, but could understand not a word. He seemed to be in a black place where, occasionally, the faces of his family would float by, out of reach, but immeasurably dear to him. He had no idea where he was, or what had happened to put him here, but his mind was too blurred to bother about that. He was aware of no time passing, as he floated in this womb of darkness – this limbo – but he just accepted that this was where he was supposed to be, for the time being.

Falconer promised to return at lunchtime to take Kerry home, and make sure she had something to eat. One of the other officers would ascertain that she got back to her husband's bedside for evening visiting. That was all he could do for now, and he turned his weary steps towards the station, to see what had happened in his absence.

It wasn't quite eleven thirty when he arrived there, and he made straight for the canteen to get something in his belly. He hadn't eaten since the evening before, and he felt husked out and completely devoid of energy.

As he wolfed down a full English and swigged tea, the very act of eating in the canteen made him think of Carmichael, and the gargantuan platefuls his partner had consumed opposite him, so recently. Even the thought of the sergeant's huge tea mug brought a lump to his throat, as he finished his meal and contemplated the possibility that Carmichael might never have breakfast with him again.

It was definitely time that he went to his office and got on with some work, but when he got there, his whole working world was turned upside down by what he saw. At Roberts' desk sat Merv Green, almost unrecognisable in civvies at the station. Under Falconer's own desk lounged a large furry rug that greeted him as if he hadn't seen him in years, and proved to be Mulligan.

'I'm sorry, sir, but I couldn't take him to mine and leave him there on his own all day. Not only would he be lonely, but he'd probably rip the place to shreds just to pass the time.'

The worst thing though, was that there was someone sitting in Carmichael's chair, at Carmichael's desk. A very large man with skin as black as the night had been poring over the sergeant's computer as the inspector had entered, and was now on his feet, standing to attention.

'Who the hell are you, and what the bloody hell are you doing sitting at my sergeant's desk?' barked Falconer, his pallid face flushing an angry purple at the sheer impertinence of the man.

As he was venting his spleen on his unsuspecting victim, there was a discreet knock at the door, and Superintendent 'Jelly' Chivers himself squeezed into the office. 'Ah, good morning, DI Falconer. I've just popped in to introduce you to DS Ngomo. He's on loan to us while both your men are hospitalised, and I've authorised PC Green to work as Acting DC until such times as your forces are back to full strength.

'I'm sure you'll find both of them hardworking and efficient, and eager to gather sufficient evidence to put those bastards who did that to DS Carmichael behind bars for a very long time.

'As officer-in-charge, I'll leave the delegation of duties up to you, knowing the case will be in secure hands. We've probably got enough evidence in that freezer alone to put them away, but I want to know the ins-and-outs of a duck's arse in this case, and I don't want any of the force to rest until we've got precisely that.

'We owe it to Carmichael and his family to see justice fully and publicly done. Well done for dealing with that murdering swine when he tried to resist arrest,' he concluded, and actually winked at Falconer. And he disappeared out of the door again as suddenly as he had entered.

'Well,' said Falconer. 'Please excuse my boorish behaviour when I arrived, Sergeant Ngomo. It was the shock of seeing someone else at my partner's desk. I had no idea that the Super had called for reinforcements.'

Still at attention, Ngomo replied, 'There was no reason for you to have known I'd be here. My Christian name is Matthew, and I have four brothers; Mark, Luke, John and Gotobed. Gotobed is, of course, not his real name, but it has stuck since he was a small child.'

'Pleased to meet you, and I am DI Falconer, and I like to be called either 'sir' or Inspector. I do not answer to the repulsive term 'guv'. What do you prefer to be called?'

'Matthew will do fine, sir. It is my given name in Jesus,' the new sergeant replied, then fell silent.

'Green, how long is this dog going to be a feature in the office?' Mulligan had held his peace while Chivers was in the room, but now he'd gone, the dog could not contain himself any longer, and was pawing and licking at Falconer furiously, while making whining noises of friendliness and joy.

'When I got in this morning, I was told to get myself into civvies and report to your office. The dog had been making a helluva row all night, barking at those two who did for Carmichael, and the duty sergeant was nearly out of his mind, so I said I'd bring him up here, take him home with me tonight, and keep him until he can go back to his owners. I'll ask around to see if there's anywhere else in the station that he can stay during working hours.'

Green could hardly suppress a wide grin, as he couldn't believe his luck, not only at being given a chance in plain clothes, albeit temporarily, but having the chance to look after this absolutely splendid dog as well.

'That's a very generous offer, to look after him yourself. Make sure you get expenses for his food and anything else he needs. I'm afraid I'm in no state to question either of those two downstairs, so I'd like you to take it turn and turnabout with them, and see what you can pry out of them.

'Me, I'm not rostered for duty today, so I'm going home. Now!' and the inspector turned on his heel, and marched out of the office, down the stairs, and out of the front door; got into his car, and drove the short distance to his home where, on reaching this sanctuary, he just collapsed on the sofa and cried as if his heart would break.

When the crying jag had ceased, he phoned the hospital, only to be told that there was no change in Carmichael's condition. He then phoned the station and explained that he was supposed to take Mrs Carmichael home from the hospital at lunchtime, but that he was temporarily incapacitated, so perhaps an unmarked car could be dispatched to drive her back to Castle Farthing.

He certainly wasn't in a fit state to transport a grieving half-widow anywhere, and he made a pot of strong coffee and settled down on the sofa to watch the two DVDs which Carmichael had so thoughtfully given him, and which he had not yet been courteous enough to watch.

He put on the wedding DVD first, and watched the guests arrive, the ceremony, then candid shots from the speeches and reception. It brought back so many memories, that he was either laughing or crying the whole way through. He even managed to laugh at a couple of scenes that showed himself, half-cut, and trying to dance to the frantic music that he barely remembered. Deciding that he ought, in future, to save himself for such old-fashioned dances as the waltz and foxtrot, he changed to the christening DVD.

From the very first scene he had a lump in his throat. Carmichael and Kerry looked like a golden couple, baby Harriet, a princess, in her Victorian goffered gown that hung nearly to the ground. (He hadn't noticed this magnificent garment before, because of his state of accidental inebriation) The two boys wore suits that matched their father's, and beamed at the camera with fearsome pride.

The phone rang, just after he had started watching, and he rose and pulled the plug from its socket, then reached into his pocket to turn off his mobile phone, too. He would watch this without interruption, as a private apology for being made a fool of by Carmichael's brothers, and missing the opportunity of joining in the celebrations with a clear mind, as a proper godfather would have done.

When the DVD finished, he put his head in his hands and sobbed out his misery, that such a thing could happen. If he hadn't been so disgusted with Honey, he wouldn't have been in such a bad mood. If he hadn't been in such a bad mood, he would have made more haste to get to Fallow Fold. And if he'd got to Fallow Fold just a couple of minutes earlier, he could have prevented what eventually happened. It was all his fault, and the weight of guilt was unbearably heavy.

After about half an hour, he poured himself a good slug of scotch, and put on the first DVD to play again. At the end of it, he put on the second one, again accompanied by an even larger slug of whisky, and that was how Doc Christmas found him, when he called round to see how he was, having heard that he'd just walked out of the station with barely a word.

It took him some while to get an answer to the door, but he persevered until Falconer got tired of the constant knocking and ringing, and flung himself out into the hall to see who was making such a nuisance of themselves. Didn't they know he was grieving? Didn't the whole world know that?

Doc Christmas was one of the few who did know in what state he was likely to find the inspector, and was ready for either fight or flight, when the man himself eventually answered this persistent summons.

Falconer looked like a tramp, and was such a lightweight as far as alcohol was concerned, and so exhausted, that he was practically incoherent after two large drinks. Brooking no argument, the doctor took him gently by the shoulders and about-turned him, pushing him in the small of the back, to get him to go back into the sitting room.

That achieved, he put on the kettle, and began rooting around in the kitchen to find something that he could cook, so that the man at least had food in his belly. 'Beans on toast do you?' he called through, only to find that Falconer was dead to the world, asleep on the sofa, and snoring like a prize porker.

He woke him to feed him, gave him two cups of scalding hot tea, then pulled out of one of his jacket pockets two small bottles. 'Get yourself upstairs and into your pyjamas, and let me know when you're in bed, and I'll come up and minister to you. Do it! Now!'

Ten minutes later, he was standing in Falconer's bedroom with a tray, on which rested a mug of hot chocolate, a pint glass of water, and two small pills, one white, the other yellow. Falconer was looking mulish about the pills but, as Doc Christmas told him, if he didn't take them immediately he'd summon Falconer's GP and tell him the man was fit only for certifying under section two of the Mental Health Act. 'And don't think we couldn't do it either. It only takes two signatures and you're in the nut hut.'

The patient took the medication reluctantly; even suffering the indignity of having to open his mouth to show that he hadn't just hidden the tablets under his tongue. As he sipped the hot chocolate, Christmas sat on the edge of the bed, and promised he'd let him know if anything at all happened, with respect to Carmichael's condition.

'You should sleep through to the morning now. I'll call in first thing, to see whether you're fit to work and, if you're not, you do what's best for you, and not what you think you should do. The world won't come to an end just because you miss a couple of days in the office. And going into work won't make Carmichael any better or worse than he was going to be anyway.'

Five minutes later, the doctor removed the mug gently from Falconer's slackening fingers and pulled the duvet over him, before tiptoeing from the room and leaving him to sleep off his grief and guilt, or as much of it as he could. He'd be back in the morning to judge his fitness for work.

Chapter Fifteen

Sunday

The doctor was true to his word, and returned on Sunday morning to Letsby Avenue to assess his patient's physical and mental state. He arrived at ten thirty bearing a bag of croissants and the enormous weight of one of the larger-circulation Sunday newspapers.

When Falconer opened the door to him, it was obvious that the inspector hadn't long been out of bed, as he was still in dressing gown and slippers, his hair was a mess of spikes, and he evidently hadn't found time, yet, for a shower.

Doc Christmas bustled in like a male nanny, organising a pot of coffee and setting the kitchen with the necessary accoutrements for them to sit down and have breakfast together. 'Have you fed the cats yet?' he asked. 'From the smell, I detect that you haven't had time to clear their litter tray. No, no; you sit down, and I'll sort everything out, then we're going to get something inside you, and you can't spend the whole day looking like a scarecrow.

'When you've eaten, showered, shaved, and dressed, we're going to sit down together, and you're going to talk about how you really feel. I don't want any of this daft stiff upper lip guff from you. For once, I want you to pour out your feelings. You'll be amazed at how cathartic it can be, and you know nothing you tell me will go any further.'

Falconer shuffled through to the kitchen, the sunlight from the window highlighting his stubbled face and the drawn expression on it. 'How is he?' he asked, knowing he had no need to identify about whom he was asking.

175

'He's holding his own, and if he regains consciousness and you look like a bucket of shite, he's not going to be very encouraged, is he? He'll think he's going to die if you look like you've gone to pieces, now start eating these croissants while I pour the coffee, then you can get up to the bathroom and turn yourself back into a human being.'

For once, Falconer did as he was told, and looked marginally better after his late breakfast. The doc then shooed him upstairs, and told him not to come down again until he'd checked in a mirror that he looked his normal respectable self. 'Then we talk,' he concluded.

Forty-five minutes later, the inspector was sitting stiffly on the edge of the sofa, willing himself to open his heart and verbalise his horror at what had happened, his fears for Carmichael's survival, and the nagging guilt that, if he hadn't been in such a filthy mood about Honey, he would have arrived at the scene more quickly and could, perhaps, have prevented what happened to Carmichael. This one aspect of the situation seemed to haunt his every waking moment.

It was a lifetime's outpouring of grief, and he was astounded at how it wracked his body. Strangely, once he'd started, he found he couldn't stop, trying to explain his shyness and loneliness, and he even gabbled out the story of why he was in a sulk in the first place, and what Honey had told him. It came out in a flood, a cataract of words that he couldn't stop, and by the time he'd finished he felt exhausted, but a little better.

'Harry,' said Doc Christmas, 'There's no way you can go back and change any of that; you don't have a time machine. What you can do is help out with Davey's wife and children, and visit him in hospital. If it helps, pray for him. I'm going to advise Chivers that, in my opinion, you're not fit to work at the moment, and recommend that he grant you a week's compassionate leave, sick leave, call

176

it what you will.

'You also must try to express your emotions, and not bottle them up inside. That way madness lies. Try to be more open about how you feel. People won't perceive that as a weakness, but rather as a strength, that you have the ability to show your vulnerable side.'

Falconer tried to interrupt, but was talked through and down.

'You will do as you're advised and I shall brook no argument. At the moment you're simply not fit to work, and you wouldn't be able to exercise sound or positive judgement on anything. I want you to take these tablets,' here he handed him a strip of anonymous pills, 'two a day, and these,' and he handed over another strip, 'one at night.

'You're not indestructible and you're not immortal. You need to eat, sleep, rest, and recuperate, just like any other human being. Do the sensible thing and take my advice on this, and you'll be feeling more able to face the world much more quickly. No, don't argue. Just do what you're told, for once in your life.'

'Yes, Nanny,' replied Falconer meekly.

'I'll call in every day to make sure that you're following instructions, and if you need to talk any more, you know you can trust me. I'm used to keeping all my patients' secrets; yours won't be too much more of a burden. But you must start learning how to express your feelings, or you'll have a complete breakdown.'

'Yes, Nanny.'

Shortly after the doctor had left, the phone rang, and Falconer found Superintendent 'Jelly' Chivers himself on the other end of the line. Without preamble, he launched straight into his lecture.

'I'm calling from the station,' – on a Sunday? – 'and I've been talking to some of the men. I've just had a brief chat with the FME, and he says he's already seen you this morning. I'm going to take the man's advice, and I'm ordering you to take a week away from work. I can't have you working on this case anyway, because you're too close to it. You've already half-killed Mr Dixon once, and I don't want a recurrence of that in my station, although this is the last time I shall ever speak of that incident.

'I've got a new team together, and I want you out of harm's way while they conduct interviews, take statements, and gather evidence. You're too closely involved, with what happened to Carmichael. Take a break; maybe go away for a couple of days. I'll be in touch.'

The inspector hadn't managed to utter a word, when Chivers rang off, and he was left standing there with the phone in his hand, wondering what would have happened if the man had dialled a wrong number. He'd never have known, not having given him the opportunity to answer or comment on anything.

He had no idea what he would do with himself with no office to go to, and then he remembered that he used to be quite a good pianist, and he'd spent quite a long time learning Greek, and had become quite proficient at it. Maybe he ought to go back a few paces and find out who he had been when he was first partnered with Carmichael.

Of course, he'd see what he could do for Kerry and the children, and spend some time at the hospital where he had two officers incarcerated, but it seemed like the 'essential' Falconer had gone astray. He seemed to have worked non-stop since the start of their partnership, and realised the possibility that he'd been driving himself a little too hard.

It was time to take his foot off the accelerator of life, and transfer it to the brake for a while. Carmichael had, in fact, been a prime example of how to balance his personal life with his professional, and Falconer had never noticed before what a fine juggling act he did. He just hoped to God that the young man had more time left in which to

178

demonstrate this skill.

That afternoon found Falconer sitting by Carmichael's bedside. He'd been told that, although his colleague was unconscious, he could probably still hear, and it might be a good idea to talk to him about incidents they had shared together.

This was not something he thought he would have considered doing in the past, but so emotional had he become at the thought that he may lose his partner, that he forced himself to remember some of the more bizarre incidents in their shared past. He also talked about some of the weird and wonderful clothing Carmichael had worn during their time together, reviewing the best part of two years, case by case.

As he sat there, thus engaged, DC Roberts wandered in from the general ward, and sat on the end of the bed to listen. He'd only been stationed in Market Darley for a few of their previous cases – and had spent most of the first one in hospital, after being beaten almost to death with a baseball bat, and the greater part of his second case in a similar condition, after being a victim of a hit-and-run accident.

This third case had seen him hospitalised before it had really got going, and he knew some of the hospital staff really well, now, and was treated rather as a pet. Listening to the inspector saved a lot of time reading notes, and was far more entertaining.

One case, over Christmas, between hospital stays but during convalescence, he had missed completely, and rocked with laughter, at the same time groaning with pain, at some of Carmichael's more ludicrous ideas, like building a hen-house inside the house, without considering how he would get such a large structure out into the garden.

At four o'clock, Kerry arrived, Roberts returned to his

ward, and Falconer discreetly ended his visit, passing a few minutes with her to discuss her husband's condition, and to enquire how things were going at home.

He had already seen the biggest get well card ever printed leaning against the wall by the sergeant's bed, and Kerry told him she had received an enormous bouquet and basket of fruit from the station, and that Bob Bryant had actually left the reception desk and come to visit her personally, to tell her how much he admired Carmichael, and how far the young man had come since moving to plain clothes. This was better than a glowing report from the superintendent himself, and she glowed with pride, as she repeated what he had said.

She also told him that the doctors had decided to allow the sedation to wear off the following day, and see how her husband reacted. The children were worried, but fine, and having Linda Starr there made all the difference. She talked her out of her misery, amused the children, and shopped for her, so that she wouldn't have to face any questions she wasn't ready for.

Merv was visiting after tea tonight, and the children had been very excited about him coming over, as he intended to bring Mulligan as well, and the thought of having two adults in the house who were not their parents, and the anticipation of rides on Mulligan's back, was enough to make them laugh with happiness – something they had not done since the attack on their father.

After leaving the hospital, Falconer went home and put together a scrappy meal for himself, before driving over to Shepford St Bernard, the village in which he and Carmichael had worked their last murder case, and attending Evensong in the church of St Bernard-in-the-Downs.

His reason for this was twofold. He found Evensong a very comforting service, full of reassurance, with an atmosphere that was timeless. He also wanted to have a word with Rev. Florrie Feldman. Her no-nonsense attitude was exactly what he felt he needed at the moment, in his precarious emotional state.

The tiny church choir sang the psalms, a tradition that he loved and always found very calming, and Rev. Florrie recognised him in the small but loyal congregation, and realised that he had probably come to the church to see her; thus, she said goodbye to the other members of the congregation, then came back into the body of the church to see him, instead of disappearing straight into the vestry to disrobe.

Falconer's worries were not just about Carmichael's survival, but about the very existence of God, and the continuing life of souls after death. He had been brought up as a regular church-goer, a tradition that was continued through both prep and boarding school.

He had taken a bit of a 'pagan break' while at university, but had become a Sunday worshipper again in the army – but since he had left that force and joined another, he was back in no-man's-land as far as his real beliefs went.

Rev. Florrie was pragmatic as ever, and he left her company with little idea of what she had really said, but strangely reassured by her words.

The inspector had been home no longer than half an hour when there was a ring on the doorbell, just as the cats were having their mad minutes, a daily occurrence in the early evening. Shutting them in the sitting room with difficulty, he opened the front door to find Merv Green on the doorstep, clutching a bottle of very good red wine and an armful of packets of snacks.

'Thought you might like some company,' he stated baldly, elbowed his way into the hall and opened the sitting room door, only to be literally bowled over by a crazy feline game of tag. Luckily, he staggered a step or two before completely overbalancing, and the bottle of wine landed safely in an armchair.

'Give me dogs every time,' he stated, then added, 'Come on, sir. Get out the corkscrew. There's a man dying of thirst here, and it isn't you.'

'Only if you tell me how the interviews are going, and what you've learnt about the Maitlands,' Falconer replied, heading for the kitchen, still surprised by Green's visit.

'Deal,' a deep voice called back from the other room, and the inspector loaded a tray with wine glasses, glass bowls for the snacks, and the all-important corkscrew.

When everything had been set out, the wine had had a minimal time to breathe, and they were settled in armchairs, Merv started the conversation, but not on the subject that Falconer had expected. 'That Ngomo's a bit of an oddball, don't you think?'

'I only saw the man for a couple of minutes, but he didn't seem like a native.'

'Oh, he's that all right, born in good old London town, but apparently his parents speak hardly any English, so all six of them chat in African lingo at home. Do you know what he asked me after you'd, er, gone on leave?'

'Enlighten me,' replied Falconer, intrigued, despite his impatience to hear about the case.

'He only went and asked me if I'd found Jesus.'

'What on earth did you say?'

'I told him I hadn't realised he was missing, but that I'd keep an eye out for him and if I hadn't found him within forty-eight hours, I'd put out a missing persons report.'

'How on earth did he react to that?'

'He just smiled that sappy smile of his, and walked away shaking his head. Did you notice his eyes?'

'I really didn't have time. Gazing into sergeants' eyes isn't one of my regular pastimes, believe it or not.'

'They're like black stones in pools of blood, they're so bloodshot. I put it down to too much praying.'

'Green!'

'Yes, sir?'

'Shut up and bring me up to date with the case.'

'Here goes. We've been taking it in turns to interview them. We were both in all day yesterday, and I went in this morning, then I went to Carmichael's place after they'd had their tea – nice kids – then I checked back at the station before I came here, because I knew you'd want an up-to-date picture of what we've discovered.'

Chapter Sixteen

Sunday Evening

'Dixon and Mrs Maitland have known each other for decades. They met in college, and were "going steady", as they used to call it, in the olden days,' Merv began his tale.

'Dixon claimed never to have loved anyone else, but then along came Melvyn Maitland, with his long hair and beard – which he still has – and swept Marilyn off her feet with his casual approach to life and his laid-back attitude. She fell for it, hook, line, and sinker, and broke up with Dixon, marrying Maitland only a couple of months later.

'Dixon was almost out of his mind with grief, and dropped out of college shortly afterwards. Meanwhile, Mrs Maitland discovered that the gypsy life was not as wonderful as she had expected. She found it very unsettling, constantly moving on, not settling anywhere, and hadn't been prepared for the fact that Maitland never intended to pay tax of any sort to any government department.

'In effect, they became what she described as "tax ghosts", always renting furnished properties, and doing a flit if it seemed that any agency was catching up with them. Maitland himself did anything and everything, provided it paid cash, but it was a precarious life that stopped her pressing for a family. If *she* didn't like the lifestyle, she felt she could hardly subject a child or children to it.

'After a couple of years, she'd had enough, and contacted Dixon, who was still living with his mother in the same house, and they became secret lovers, only meeting infrequently in cheap hotels and boarding houses, but their meetings gave them both something to look forward to. Maitland wasn't a fool, though, and he noticed when Marilyn suddenly started to be in a better mood, seeming happier than she'd been for quite a long time.

'It didn't take him long to find evidence of her adulterous activities, in the form of a clutch of letters from Dixon, declaring his undying love, and which she should have burnt, but couldn't bring herself to confine to the flames.

'That was the point that Maitland began to blackmail Dixon, whose mother was a fervent Christian, and would have cut him out of her will had she known what he was doing. So weak was he that he paid up, and continued to pay up until he moved to Fallow Fold and Maitland lost track of him.

'He thought he was safe, and couldn't believe his good and his bad luck when Marilyn and Melvyn moved into the self-same village. Of course, they couldn't resist the opportunities for clandestine meetings, when Melvyn was off working somewhere else or doing deals, but he'd clocked Dixon as well.

'He wasn't a stupid man, by any means, and just presented himself on Dixon's doorstep one day with his hand held out, just like before. Even though Dixon's mother was dead by then, she had instilled her moral values in him so thoroughly, that the thought of all and sundry knowing that he was having a relationship with a married woman was anathema to him, and he began to pay again.

'Then Marilyn suggested a plan to him, whereby they could be together forever.'

'I say, Merv, you've got a jolly good storytelling style when you put your mind to it,' interrupted Falconer.

'Well, I'm not down the pub with me mates now, am I, and Twinkle wants me to talk better. She thinks it'll help me get on in the force,' he replied with a rueful smile.

'She's probably right, too. Keep it up. Now, on you go.'

'She'd managed to winkle out of Melvyn that it was he who did all that vandalism when he was stinking drunk. He was the co-ordinator for all the groups, and he'd had a bit of a time of it with them lately. He got absolutely rat-arsed one night and attacked the property of some of the people he thought were responsible for all the extra work he'd had to do.

'Then there was that attack on the German bloke, and she thought they could make use of those incidents to stage Dixon's disappearance, after leaving an unbelievable note mentioning his dead mother. Then, a couple of days later, if no one had accused Melvyn of doing away with him, he could come back, clandestinely, and she and Dixon would do away with Melvyn and hide his body in the freezer. It's just a pity that the freezer was rather too small, and they had to dismember him.

'Marilyn had also forgotten her passport, then thought that Melvyn's might be handy too. They might be able to sell it to some unscrupulous individual if they ran short of funds, and Dixon had already been back once for his own. They were holed-up in a bed and breakfast place in Carsfold while they were plotting their departure.

'Neither of them will say when they did for Melvyn, but Doc Christmas says there's a knife wound in the neck which would have severed the jugular. They were probably both there when it happened, and can you imagine the scene, with Maitland with a knife sticking out of his neck, blood spurting everywhere, and him staggering round the utility room, roaring and pulling at the knife? God, it'd really have pulsed out when he removed the plug. And they probably just looked on, too frightened to move.'

He stopped momentarily, and shuddered. 'Anyway,

whenever it was, we know when they came back to cut him up just as if he were a sheep or a cow, and stuff the bits in the freezer.'

'But what about the blood we found on the fireplace in Dixon's house? Was it Dixon's after all, or was it Maitland's, left there by accident as it were?'

'It *was* Dixon's. Apparently he always sharpens his pencils with a pen-knife, and cut himself, sharpening one so that the shavings went into the fireplace and didn't make a mess of the floor.'

'You couldn't make this up! So the mention of his mother was deliberate?'

'It certainly was. He knew he'd told people that she'd died, and that someone would say something sooner or later. They might even think he'd been coerced into writing it by someone who didn't know about her death. That would have been even better, because with him gone, and then Maitland disappearing, Maitland would probably have been suspected of doing away with his neighbour, and the two love-birds would have the chance to flee the country to start a new life together, before anyone was actively looking for them.

'No one would be looking for a couple. They'd eventually find Maitland's dismembered body, but his wife would be well away by then, and maybe they'd even have the opportunity for Mrs M. to make an honest man of Mr D., somewhere abroad.'

'Some people really make life difficult for themselves,' Falconer commented. 'If only he'd had the guts to ask her to leave her husband, none of this would have happened, and they could have lived happily ever after, in sin. Morals sometimes cause more trouble than they're worth.' This was something that he had never expected to hear coming from his own mouth, and he realised he had been reassessing his ideals and opinions since that murderous attack on Carmichael.

It didn't change the way he felt about Honey one whit, for he had felt sure that they had established the basis of a soon-to-be-realised relationship in the time they had known each other. He had been absolutely certain that she felt the same way about him as he felt about her. In the light of what she'd done, he was either very wrong, or she was simply not the person he thought she was, nor the right person for him.

Suddenly realising that there was a character missing from the scenario, he asked, 'Where's Mulligan this evening? Not out on the tiles, I hope.'

'I dropped him off at mine with a nice juicy bone. The thought of that well-meaning monster with your pride of cats, was just too horrible to contemplate, so I gave him a huge meal, then the bone, and left him to sleep it off when he'd finished chewing. That said, I'd better get back to him, or he'll start eating the furniture.'

'But there's still half a bottle of this glorious wine left.' Falconer had enjoyed the company, and was loth for his guest to leave.

'Put the cork back in. It'll keep for another day. Are you going in to see Carmichael tomorrow? I hear Roberts will be discharged in a couple of days, so you could kill two birds with one stone.'

'I think I'll do just that. I understand the doctor's will be stopping the sedation after tonight, so I'll leave it until late afternoon in the hope that he's regained consciousness.'

Monday

Falconer slept well that night, but whether it was from a slightly calmer frame of mind, or from the effects of the tablets Doc Christmas had given him, he had no idea. He did feel a little more optimistic, however, and realised that his outlook on life had been changed by recent events.

He had always felt very alone. An only child, he had not mixed well at school, spent his time at university studying, and been called aloof in the army, and there had been no change in him since he had joined the police force.

He was not close to his parents, who knew the price of everything and the value of nothing, and spent their time flitting from dinner party to cocktail party, without a thought for anyone outside their immediate social circle; and he was not included in that, although from choice rather than neglect. For them, it was 'out of sight, out of mind', and he was very dilatory about keeping in touch.

The behaviour of his police colleagues had made him realise that he was *not* on his journey alone, though. Every officer who knew Carmichael had made some sort of contribution, either with physical help, as with the donation of their own blood, or with the collection that he knew Bob Bryant was making for the injured sergeant's family. There were dozens of signatures on that huge get well card, from the part-time clerks to the superintendent himself.

Their thoughtfulness about his own well-being was touching, too. Finally he realised that he did have friends, and good ones. Sometimes one's family was comprised of people who weren't blood relatives, but who had adopted one into their circle out of sheer kindness. The force was his real family, and Carmichael was like the little (!) brother he never had, although one who still thought he was Peter Pan, and refused to grow up.

He was godfather to the Carmichaels' three children, and even their dogs loved him. Granted he'd thought of his cats as his family, but now he knew better, and looked further than the four walls of his own home for this blessing.

Basking in this revelation, he was startled when the phone rang, and even more alarmed when he answered its urgent summons. Kerry was on the other end of the phone, sobbing her heart out. His blood ran cold.

'No!' he almost shouted. 'No, no, no, no, no!'

'No,' she replied, getting back a modicum of self-control. 'No, he's all right, really. I'm just crying with relief. He's conscious, and he seems to be OK.'

'What makes you say that?' Falconer asked, thinking that Kerry was no medical expert, and might just be pinning her hopes on the fact that he had squeezed her hand, or something equally inconclusive and trivial.

'He asked me to bring something in for him.'

'What?'

'His Beano annuals. He said his Dandy ones could come in in a couple of days as he wanted his favourites first.'

'He really is all right, isn't he?'

'Yes, thank God!'

'Hallelujah, praise the Lord. Amen. I'll be going in to see him this afternoon. Is there anything you suggest I bring in for him?'

'Some comics, until I can get there later. He'll be bored to death, having to lie there with nothing to do and nothing to read.'

'Done!'

Falconer turned up promptly for afternoon visiting, and found his sergeant propped up in bed and looking much better, although he was still attached to various monitors.

'I'm so glad you're going to be fine. You really had me worried, there,' admitted Falconer, not usually this communicative about how he felt. 'At first, I thought you were a goner, and so did the surgeon, if he were honest.'

'So did I, sir. I was never so frightened in all my life as when that man came at me with that fork. I don't really remember much after that, except being in a completely dark place, with the sensation of floating. Sometimes I saw the faces of my family float by, but most of the time I just floated there, and didn't feel at all worried about anything. I had no idea where I was, but I'm sure glad to be back here, and not dead.'

'You're not the only one.'

'What have you got in that carrier bag, sir? Is it something for me?' asked Carmichael, hoping that it was.

Falconer handed over his cache and the patient whooped, as best he could, at the bundle that was passed to him. 'Comics! You know me better than I thought, sir.'

'And you won't have to have a tattoo done, now. You've probably got a rather exclusive one right across your middle,' commented the inspector.

'I'll probably end up looking like a dot-to-dot puzzle, and the boys will want to join them to see what they make,' Carmichael replied.

'And with an indelible marker,' Falconer concluded.

Not to be outdone, Carmichael piped up with, 'Hey, I can do a trick with this equipment. Watch this, sir.'

With that, he pulled out one of the connections of the machine that was monitoring his heartbeat, and the spiky line suddenly stopped spiking, and an alarm went off. 'Look, sir,' he exhorted the inspector. 'Flat line!' Then he hastily pushed it back into its connection and assumed an expression of innocence, as the sound of running feet became audible.

Falconer, who would, in the past, have been extremely censorious of such an irresponsible action, had no time to conjure up a stern lecture, as he was too busily engaged, in the middle of a huge belly laugh.

THE END

P.S. Anyone concerned with the fate of the litter of 'Chihua-shire' pups may rest assured that Kerry Carmichael re-homed them via a Carsfold vet, so that each could obtain the love and attention they deserved, and which there simply wouldn't be time for in the caring but chaotic Carmichael household.

Author's note: The return of Mulligan is in response to a request from my husband, who loves the antics of the humongous fictional hound. When he gets that gleam in his eye, however, I don't worry too much, as I'm allergic to dogs, an d our six cats would definitely disapprove if he turned up here with the huge bulk of a Great Dane pup.

Happy reading!

An Excerpt From

Glass House

The Falconer Files: Book 11

by

Andrea Frazer

PROLOGUE

Fairmile Green was a visually unusual village for more than one reason. Not only had all the shops that formed its small commercial sector been saved from demolition about a decade ago, and sympathetically restored, thus presenting the casual shopper with two rows of parallel-facing establishments with thatched roofs and timbered walls, but they were now trading as such unexpected businesses as a burger bar, sandwich shop, and £1 shop.

Most surprisingly, it had a juvenile section of the local river Darle, unimaginatively named the Little Darle, running between these two rows of commercial establishments; well-protected, of course, due to health and safety regulations, but a magnet for inquisitive children and thirsty dogs. With this charming rivulet dividing the village, the main thoroughfare was almost the widest in Britain, although the western side was named Market Street, the eastern, High Street. However, it did create a marvellously open view for the houses that ran across the end of these, as Stoney Cross Road turned left at this point, and Smithy Lane, right, thus ending the length of the thoroughfare at the southern end.

This infant river, which gave so much character to the village centre, eventually ran off underground under the property at the end of its main street, under a house which had for years been known as The Orchards.

Behind each of its rows of shops there was a little yard; the Bear Pit Yard behind the western shops, and Darley Old Yard behind the eastern. The tiny hamlet of Darley, long ago disappeared into the mists of time, was remembered thus, as only a minuscule commercial cul-de-sac in another village, and with Market Darley, a town that had survived to carry the name, only about two-and-a-half miles away in an east-north-easterly direction.

Its even tenor of life was disturbed by the annual summer influx of tourists who wanted to photograph its almost sickening quaintness, and Fairmile Green had also been reluctantly enlivened by extensive works being carried out on the largest house in the village – the one underneath which the Little Darle disappeared.

Although the landlord of The Goat and Compasses didn't mind the hustle and bustle of extra trade, the villagers resented this intrusion on the rhythm of their lives, and looked forward to the completion of the building work, and the return of the hordes of tourists and their attendant children back to school, come September.

The largest house in Fairmile Green stood at the southern end of the village and had, as mentioned, always been called The Orchards. This building had once owned the whole frontage across both Market Street and High Street but, at some time in the first part of the twentieth century, the owner at the time had sold off little parcels of land for which the relevant authority was only too glad to grant planning permission, not wanting the village to die, as so many others were doing.

Thus, the big house now shared this enviable view down the centre of the village with half a dozen other residences, that particular owner of The Orchards being canny enough to sell only shallow plots, and having the stroke of brilliance to build a wall across all of the new boundaries, sacrificing only a few of the trees that made up the magnificent orchard that had been established to the rear of the property, and after which it had been named.

The house was just a little bit too young to be a listed building, but old enough to be dilapidated, having stood empty for the best part of a decade. The first sign that it had been sold had appeared nearly a year ago. There had been no For Sale sign, nor had there been a Sold sign, but the name-plates on the gate and the front of the house had suddenly been noticed not to be there any more, and a contractor's sign had been erected in the front garden.

That was the signal that something was afoot, closely followed by what was a positive storm of activity, with vehicles belonging to a plethora of trades visiting; there had been plumbers, electricians, general builders, glaziers, landscape gardeners, professional designers, kitchen specialists, flooring specialists, and interior and exterior decorators, none of whom had been local.

The name of the new owner was the best kept secret for miles around, and the locals speculated that, if it was someone famous, then a lot of money must have changed hands to maintain this level of discretion, and this amount of renovation.

When the whirlwind of activity – which lasted for about four months – ceased, the delivery vans began to arrive, bearing the names of some very select retailers, on their sides. The new owner of The Orchards must have considerable funds to have ordered from such august names.

At last, just a month or two ago, the owner himself had turned up with a man in navy overalls who was there to fit the new name-plate for the front wall, which read, simply 'Glass House'. So that's who it was! News spread like wildfire. They were going to have Chadwick McMurrough living amongst them.

McMurrough was the current media darling, having won the television competition *The Glass House*, in which twenty people were housed in a building with glass external walls, and were filmed twenty-four hours a day. With the exception of the lavatories and bathrooms, everything they did or said was filmed, recorded, edited, then broadcast to a gullible public so that they would evict the candidates one-by-one.

The bias for the series that had been broadcast the previous year had been towards a flamboyant character who was openly and outrageously gay, with the name Chadwick McMurrough. He was outrageous not only in his opinions, but in his dress, and the outré colours and styles he wore made the editors and production team swing wildly in his favour as winner, manipulating the footage to achieve their goal.

After the programme finished, apart from the monetary award for winning such a puerile programme, McMurrough was given a short-term part in the country's favourite soap opera, *Cockneys*, and the press began to dub him 'the gay, multi-coloured thespian'.

So charismatic and bizarre was the winner, that he was offered his own chat show on one of the minor television channels in a late slot on Friday evenings. Not surprisingly, given the level of taste of the average viewer, it had become cult viewing, and McMurrough a celebrity, albeit probably a fleeting one.

The new name of the house was a mystery to anyone who had not seen the rear of the property, thought only to refer to the show that had made all this possible, but sight of the back wall revealed that its main constituent was glass; it wasn't just an homage to the show that had been his first '*milch* cow', but a means of fully enjoying the view of the orchard, for which McMurrough had secret plans.

The rear now boasted a slight extension which made it possible to have a balcony right across the back, behind which was the newly positioned master suite. This opened right out on to the balcony with multi-fold glass doors, and convincingly produced the feeling of the outside coming right into the house.

Similarly, downstairs, the new boundary of the ground floor had a similar window which, when open, gave the same effect to what Chadwick insisted on calling the lounge, much to Radcliffe's disgust. There was a slight break in this, and then yet another folding set of glass doors across the rear of the enormous kitchen/breakfast room.

At the front of the house where the dining room was situated, a huge picture window had been installed, and a specially made wooden-slatted blind hung suspended, ready to provide privacy when McMurrough entertained, although given his gregarious and extrovert character, he would probably not lower when entertaining, thus bringing back memories of his time in *The Glass House*, and his guests a taste of what it was like to be constantly on view.

To be thus displayed lifted McMurrough's spirits, as it was through this high visibility that he had made his current reputation and money, and he wished to continue with this style of life for as long as possible by being as eccentric as he could, to catch the imagination of the media. He definitely had hidden shallows.

He also had a hidden temper as well, as was publicly displayed on the day they moved in, arriving in a sporty little car behind a van that seemed to have brought their personal bits and pieces.

One item was long and thin, and was pulled from the van by Chadwick, only to have his new partner, Bailey Radcliffe, round on him in anger. 'Mind how you handle that. It's got my rods in it. You know I want to take advantage of being out in the countryside to do a bit more fishing. It'll give you a bit of time to yourself for your first love – yourself.'

The couple had become an item when McMurrough was doing his short stint in *Cockneys*, as Radcliffe was one of the directors, and they had appeared a thoroughly odd couple given how many years – nay, decades – older than McMurrough was this new beau. After so many years 'in the business', he was totally unfazed by his younger partner's current celebrity and carried on his rant without even pausing for breath.

'And don't you dare touch my fly cases. The last time you picked up one of those, it was in a terrible muddle when I opened it up. I can't think what you did with it – treated it as a maraca and gave it damned good shake?'

'Oh, unpack it your damned self,' replied Chadwick, storming off up the garden path and going into the house in a huff.

Chapter One

Monday
Market Darley

It was high summer, and the whole country seemed to be drowning in children. The streets were awash with them to such an extent that they spilled, with their parents, by necessity, it seemed, into what had previously been quiet havens of sanctuary, pub gardens and other usually 'adults only' areas.

Their mass release from their hitherto enforced studies had turned these preciously peaceful havens of privacy and tranquillity into places akin to bear-gardens, and there was no escape from their shrill and irritating presence. Thus thought DI Harry Falconer, this beautiful summer's day as he made his way back from lunch, via the bakery, to his office.

He felt as though he were wading waist-deep through a sea of dwarves, feeling as though he were part of a fairy-tale, but probably not one with a happy ending. Before the schools reopened at the end of the long summer holidays, there would, no doubt, have been several incidents either involving or caused by this river of short humanity.

He had nipped out for a ploughman's lunch today, in anticipation of the return of his DS, 'Davey' Carmichael, who had been on sick leave for so long it felt like for ever, after a near-fatal attack on him during a previous case a couple of months before.

Falconer had struggled through this time with a temporary replacement, DS Ngomo and for a short while, in the absence of DC Roberts, recovering from acute appendicitis, PC Merv Green was temporarily elevated to a plainclothes DC, much to his fiancée, PC 'Twinkle' Starr's, delight. She had ambitions for her man, and these did not include staying in uniform for the rest of his working life.

Ngomo was now safely back where he belonged and in the past, Merv had gone back into uniform, much to his secret delight, and Carmichael was coming back this afternoon.

Although Falconer had visited his colleague when he was in hospital, and many times since he had returned home to recuperate from his dreadful injury, he felt strangely nervous about resuming their partnership.

The attack on Carmichael had focused the inspector's mind on his attitudes to life and people, and had made him more human, more emotional and, ultimately, more vulnerable. He must not wrap Carmichael in cotton wool. The attack had been a dreadful stroke of bad luck for which Falconer had no need whatsoever to feel guilty, and he mustn't think it was about to happen again.

Fairmile Green

'Peacocks?' queried Bailey Radcliffe, his voice rising at the idiocy of the idea. '*Peacocks*? You bought some *peacocks*? You actually *bought* some peacocks? What do *you* know about bloody peacocks, dipstick?'

'Oh, shut your face, you old queen,' replied Chadwick McMurrough to his partner of several weeks now. 'I've always wanted some, from when I was little, and now I can afford them. So I bought some, OK?'

'No, it's not OK,' Radcliffe snapped back at him. 'Do you realise the noise the damned things make? And what do they eat? Do you know how to look after them?'

'Of course I don't, but I can look it up on the internet, and if you don't like the noise you can always wear earplugs. Anyway, I've sent the delivery guy round to the orchard where he can let them out, and we'll just have to see how it goes. He's brought a little wooden house as well, for them to sleep in, or something.'

As he finished speaking, a high-pitched cry of what sounded like 'help' sounded from the rear of the house, and Radcliffe stared at his younger partner with an 'I told you so' expression on his face.

'See, stupid, you can even hear them through double glazing.'

'I see what you mean,' agreed McMurrough, and then added doubtfully, 'I suppose we'll get used to it. Eventually. Is it just swans that only the Queen's allowed to eat, or does the rule apply to peacocks too?'

'Well, if they get on my wick sufficiently, *this* queen's going to eat the little sods. No doubt you paid a fortune for them, too?'

'It's my money.'

'Well, maybe you need some therapy before you buy anything else daft. I don't want to get back here one day and find the garden full of bloody giraffes and the like.'

'Don't be ridiculous. Why would I want giraffes?'

'Maybe you fancied them, too, when you were little, or maybe you thought they'd keep the tops of the fruit trees tidy. How would I know? You've got such a weird mind.'

'Hmph!' McMurrough made a gruesome face at his significant other and flounced out of the room to view his new acquisitions, calling back over his shoulder, 'You wait to see what's next,' in a triumphant tone of voice.

Market Darley

Falconer had left DC Roberts back at the office blowing up balloons, and Merv and PC Starr hanging a 'welcome home' banner. His job was to collect a tray of cream cakes from the bakery in the market square and convey it back to complete the preparations for Carmichael's return, and these he now conveyed up the stairs to the CID office, ready for the hero's welcome that his sergeant so richly deserved after all he had been through in the last few months.

The banner had been affixed so that it was the first thing the DS would see when he came through the door, and the two PCs had vacated the room for the canteen, to have a little light lunch before attacking the pastries a little later. Roberts was surrounded by balloons, but they were on the floor, lying like a clutch of multi-coloured aliens' eggs, instead of tied into small groups and affixed to the ceiling. Roberts himself was slumped over his desk huffing and puffing as if he had just run a marathon.

'What the hell's the matter with you, and why aren't these things strung up?' barked Falconer, his temper, as always with Roberts, as short as a winter's day.

'I'm wiped out with all that blowing up, guv'nor,' replied Roberts, playing for sympathy he was never likely to elicit from this particular source. 'I think I may be developing asthma.'

'What did you just call me?' asked Falconer, ignoring the DC's plight.

'Sorry. Sir!' replied Roberts, realising he was on to a loser here. 'I'll just get the string and tape and get it finished.'

'You'd better. He'll be here in a few minutes. Get a move on! And no stringing one long one with two round ones and going for the "are-they-really-rude, I-simply-didn't-realise" look. And there's no more sick leave for you for the next ten years after all the time you've taken off since you came here. I want to make that crystal clear.'

'You can't accuse me of swinging the lead. I was in hospital on all three of those occasions,' replied Roberts in a hurt voice.

'So you say,' said Falconer acidly.

Fortunately, they were interrupted at that moment, by

the sound of cheering from downstairs, and the sound of a number of feet on the stairs. 'He's here!' declared Falconer, beaming from ear to ear and forgetting about his beef with the DC.

The less colourful – sometimes – brother of the Jolly Green Giant loped into the room with a beam of pure pleasure to be back where he belonged, and Falconer rushed forward to pump his hand so hard that Carmichael winced, and suddenly the office was bursting with people, all welcoming back one of their own, who had come so close to losing his life in service to the Force.

By the end of the afternoon, everything felt back to normal and, as Falconer drove home, he suddenly remembered he was having dinner with a friend on Wednesday evening, a fact he had completely forgotten in his preoccupation with Carmichael's return.

Once a fortnight he shared an evening meal with Heather Antrobus, a nurse he had met while visiting his DS in hospital. She had been involved in his day-to-day nursing, and she and Falconer often met by the sergeant's bedside. They also crossed paths in the hospital canteen where Falconer often ate when visiting, and she was trying to catch a brief meal-break.

Inevitably, they had talked about her patient, and he found her both intelligent and possessed of a sense of humour that was just about identical to his own. She was half-Irish, short, and a little on the plump side, with copper beech-coloured hair and impish green eyes, and he enjoyed her company enormously.

When Carmichael had been discharged to convalesce at home, she and Falconer had agreed to meet outside duty hours whenever possible, for a simple supper and agreeable conversation, and he looked forward eagerly to these occasions. Not only did they distract him from bitter memories of a woman who had entered his life briefly and almost destroyed it, but he always felt on top of the world afterwards, putting this down to the good laugh they always shared with these meals.

Fairmile Green

McMurrough and Radcliffe were sitting in the drawing room of Glass House with the television blaring loudly in the corner to try to block out the cries of their new charges, or rather, as Radcliffe preferred to think of them, as Chadwick's latest little follies.

He was aware that his partner had already realised that maybe he'd made a tiny error of judgement by locating these screaming monsters on his own property, but he was as stubborn as a mule, and it would be some time before he got around to admitting he had made a mistake.

'Come along, Dr Doolittle,' Radcliffe shouted, above the unholy racket of the television at loud volume, in competition with the peacocks establishing their new territory. 'Let's go down the pub. At least with the fruit machines, video games, and jukebox it'll be quieter down there.'

'Point taken,' replied McMurrough. 'Although we haven't actually been inside it to see what it's like, yet.'

'Well, this feels like just the right opportunity to find out. Get your shoes on and we'll mince down there. I'll just nip upstairs and change my shirt, and I'll meet you outside.'

The Goat and Compasses was right at the other end of the High Street, and as they strolled down to it they could still hear the cries for help from the back of Glass House. 'This isn't going to endear you to the neighbours,' opined Radcliffe, and with a sorrowful shake of the head, McMurrough had to agree with him, although he still asserted his right to keep whatever pets he chose to.

The pub had no jukebox, no video games, and no fruit machines and was, in fact, a haven of calm. It was only early evening and there were few customers. The tables outside were deserted, but the couple chose to drink inside, where the incessant high-pitched cries were inaudible.

The interior was just what a village pub should be, with shining horse-brasses, copper pots and pans, and a variety of pint pots belonging to regulars, hanging up behind the highly polished bar. They didn't manage more than a couple of gin-and-tonics each before they were thoroughly rattled by the complaints of every customer who came in, having a good old moan with the landlord about the mysterious cries that were now audible from every corner of the village.

What the two new arrivals had failed to notice was that those already present in the bar, and those that arrived after them, gave the newcomers a long, hard, staring at, then went into little huddles of two or three, commenting in lowered tones on the 'odd couple' who were drinking in the corner.

'Have you seen the colours that younger one's wearing? A pink shirt and custard yellow trousers aren't, in my opinion, suitable for a nice respectable pub like this. And I'm sure I know his face from somewhere, but I can't put my finger on where.'

'That older one's wearing a toupee. That's completely undignified, if you know what I mean. Me, I just run the razor over mine when I'm shaving. There's nothing wrong in being bald.'

'Aren't they the ones that have moved into The Orchards?'

'Oh, it's not called that any more. That name mustn't have been good enough for them. They've got a new sign with "Glass House" on it; a big one – etched glass or something similarly fanciful, as if wood wasn't good enough for them, like it is for the rest of us!'

The two residents of the village, aware only of the complaints about the noise, which were not spoken quite *sotto voce*, sipped their drinks, oblivious to these other complaints expressed in more hushed tones.

Returning home before dusk, they entered the house only to find a peacock in the hall, and peacock shit on the brand new white shag-pile carpet. The first verbal response was from McMurrough, who said shamefacedly, 'Oh God, I'm sorry!'

'This is down to you, is it?' asked Radcliffe, wrinkling his nose in distaste.

'I went outside to scatter some of that feed that was brought with them when you were upstairs changing your shirt,' he explained. 'I must have left the wall open.' This wasn't as daft as it sounded, for what would have been patio doors in any other house, were extremely over-sized in this one, to aid the illusion of a glass wall.

'You mean they've been able to get in since we went out?' asked his partner, aghast.

''Fraid so. Sorry.'

'You will be. They've probably crapped all over the place. I just hope they're no good at doing stairs: terrible stain to shift, peacock poo.'

'Is it?' asked McMurrough with horror.

'How the hell should I know? I've never had peacocks in my life, but I bet the stains are just about indelible. Now, I'll get those doors shut and locked, and you can check there aren't any of those superannuated chickens upstairs doing ghastly things in our room.'

As Radcliffe closed and locked the huge doors, there was a thump, and a series of thuds accompanied by a scream.

Market Darley

Falconer got a call from Bob Bryant at the station about ten o'clock, informing him that there had been what the caller described as 'an attempt on his partner's life', out at

Fairmile Green. The partner was some sort of celebrity and, after disturbing Superintendent Chivers at home, he had been advised to use senior officers, and not send out uniformed PCs. 'Jelly', as he was known, was very sensitive to anything media-related, and was wary of being portrayed in a bad light, if he didn't send someone of sufficient rank to attend the incident.

Taking down the address as Glass House, High Street, Fairmile Green, Falconer gave Carmichael a call, just to check that he was feeling up to going out late in the evening. If not, he would have to take Roberts, and he didn't fancy that one little bit; certainly not with a celebrity involved, as Roberts would probably be star-struck and do something embarrassing like ask for an autograph.

Carmichael was, however, feeling fit and raring to go. He'd been bored out of his mind during his convalescence, and couldn't wait to get involved with a new case. 'Are you OK to drive?' asked Falconer, beginning to behave like a mother hen. It was only a trip of two-and-a-half miles for him, but more like ten for Carmichael.

'Of course I'm OK to drive. How do you think I got to the station today? Give me the address and a ten-minute start, and I'll meet you outside the property.'

After a minute or two, Falconer found that he could not face another eight minutes of pacing the floor getting paranoid about something else happening to his sergeant, and set off early; thus he was already parked up when Carmichael's battered and rusting old Skoda pulled out of Stoney Cross Road and crossed Market Street to where the inspector's Boxster was already waiting for him.

As the two men locked their cars, Falconer said, 'I must have got here quicker than I anticipated,' not only to make Carmichael think he'd only just arrived, but to cover his own embarrassment at being such a worry-guts. It would never do for Carmichael to realise his boss was turning into an old woman.

'It looks like this place has had a bit of work done on it,' commented the younger man, as Falconer rang the bell, then started with surprise as the clearly recognisable but, at present, unidentifiable theme tune of a television programme rang out in tinkling form.

The door was answered by a man somewhere in his late forties or early fifties wearing a good, but not that good, wig, and an expression that denoted extreme anxiety. Without preamble, this study in fear informed them, 'They must have got in when we were down the pub. Forget-Me-Not forgot to close the back doors, and anyone could have got in. It's a miracle we weren't cleaned out at the same time, but setting a booby trap was just spiteful.'

'Why don't we go inside, and we can talk about whatever's happened a little more calmly,' suggested Falconer, moving to insert his foot over the door jamb.

'Oh, where are my manners,' replied the, for the moment, unidentified man in the toupee, and preceded them into a sumptuous drawing room, the back wall of which was almost entirely made of glass.

'Nice place you've got here,' commented Falconer, while Carmichael just stood, his mouth agape, catching flies.

'Nice of you to say so,' replied their host. 'By the way, I'm Bailey Radcliffe, and my partner, Chadwick McMurrough, is upstairs having a little lie down. It was he, you see, who was the victim of this attempted murder.'

'Chadwick McMurrough?' squeaked Carmichael. '*The Glass House*? *Cockneys*? *Chadwick's Chatterers*?'

'That's right. Are you a fan?' Radcliffe was interested to find out. He was much more at ease now the cavalry had arrived.

'He really makes me laugh,' replied Carmichael, his face breaking out into a wide grin. 'I've been in hospital, then convalescing at home, and his programme was one of the things that kept me sane. He asks such outrageous questions, and the looks on his guests' faces when he does is priceless.'

It was now Falconer's mouth that gaped open in surprise that his sergeant should watch such candyfloss pap.

They were almost immediately distracted, however, by the pattering of slippered feet down the stairs, and Chadwick McMurrough, in the flesh, tripped – although not literally, this time – through the door, his face wreathed in smiles as he approached the policemen with his hand outstretched.

McMurrough, being the sort of person he was, had already crept down as soon as they had been admitted, and had been shamelessly eavesdropping, before creeping back to the landing, from whence he had descended for a second time, but with a slightly heavier tread.

Falconer shook the outstretched hand briefly, but Carmichael almost curtsied in honour, as he pumped the minor celebrity's hand for rather longer than appeared necessary or appropriate, as introductions were made.

'Shall we get down to business then, gentlemen?' queried Falconer, feeling slightly queasy at the hero-worship in Carmichael's eyes, and Radcliffe waved them towards a pair of white sofas that proved to be feather-stuffed, something that Falconer didn't discover until he sank so far down into one that his knees were almost round his ears. Carmichael looked even more ridiculous, given his enormous height.

McMurrough took one look at the sergeant and said, a wicked smile lighting up his face, 'My, they breed 'em big round here for the Force, don't they? Tell me, are there any more at home like you?'

Although Carmichael was married now and had two step-children and one of his own, his mind still flew back to the chaotic over-crowded nest that had been his childhood home.

Carmichael merely gulped, then croaked, 'Yes. Lots,' in reply, thinking how jealous his brothers, and possibly his sisters too, would feel when they found out that he had met – actually met – the famous Chadwick McMurrough.

Radcliffe interrupted, saying, 'Don't tease the poor man, Chaddy. He's not used to you and your wicked comments,' but McMurrough, so easily distracted, was now watching with great enjoyment how Carmichael was going to be able to manipulate his pen and notebook, when his knees were higher than his nose.

'Would you care to sit in a more upright chair?' asked Radcliffe with a sigh of exasperation, as he watched McMurrough snicker behind his hand at the incongruous sight of what looked like a stork trying to take notes.

Carmichael finally settled on an upright, very trendy, wooden chair. Falconer asked, with some frustration in his voice at the delay, 'Do you think we could get on with what actually happened.? I'm sure you gentlemen want to get off to bed as much as we do,' then blushed a rich crimson as he examined, in retrospect, what he had just said, conscious of a hastily suppressed snigger from McMurrough, who had also seen the interpretation that could be applied to the inspector's words.

'Shut up, Chaddy, and leave the poor policemen alone. I'll do the talking, for now, if you don't mind, Mr Gobby.'

They got no further than this before there was a cry of 'help' in a female pitch of voice, from the garden, and Carmichael shot up from his chair and raced to the rear glass doors, scrabbling at the mechanism to open them.

'Leave it, Sergeant,' advised Radcliffe with a sigh of exasperation. 'It's only a peacock. They do sound awfully human, but it was soft lad here's idea to get them, so he can work out what to do with them. They're driving me out of my mind already, and they only arrived earlier today.'

Carmichael re-took his seat, his face now as red as the inspector's, at this monumental gaffe. What did he know of peacocks? They were moving in high circles here, and no mistake. When he'd set off for the station just after lunch, he had had no idea he'd be hobnobbing with a celebrity before bedtime.

'Now, I'll tell this,' began Radcliffe, with a glare at McMurrough, 'up to the time that our little victim fell down the stairs, then it's up to you what you want to do about it, Officers. We went out for a drink earlier, to get away from the awful sound from out back. Just before we left, I went upstairs to change my shirt, not knowing soft lad here had gone out into the garden to throw some food for those screaming monsters. Guess who forgot to close the doors properly and lock them?

'We didn't discover this until we got back, and all seemed to be well, so we locked up, and my significant other here went trotting off upstairs. The next thing I knew there was this awful girly scream, and he bounced down the whole flight like a lead balloon, a positive rainbow in motion.

'Once I'd got him on his feet and given him his dummy dipped in gin to pacify him, I had a look to see what he'd stumbled over, and there was a trip-wire stretched across the staircase, two steps down from the top. It could only have been put there while we were out at the pub, and only be made possible because Chaddy forgot to lock up.

'To my mind, that indicates that we were being watched, and the fact that whoever it was, was able to get in, was just by the purest bad luck, for us – or rather, for him over there; the one covered in bruises, I don't think! Any ideas how we go about tracking down whodunit?

'To my mind, this was no practical joke. He could easily have been killed, or broken his neck and been paralysed. And, with such a serious attempt to harm him, I'm pretty positive that whoever it is will try again.'

'I'll get someone over to dust for prints and look for any sign of an intruder in the rear garden. We'll also need your fingerprints for elimination purposes – I'm sure you understand why.

'I can also increase the frequency with which a patrol car passes through the village, making sure that they have an extra good look at the exterior of your property, but apart from that, there's nothing else we can do. There simply isn't the manpower to put someone on permanent guard,' said Falconer glumly, hoping that this so-called celebrity didn't use his fifteen minutes of fame to set the press on to them.

'Well, I suppose that'll have to do, for now, but if there's any further nonsense – maybe injury – I shall have to get on to a private security firm for protection. In the meantime, I'll get Chadwick to order the installation of CCTV coverage of the outside, so that if anything else occurs, we'll at least have some evidence to put forward.'

Radcliffe was sounding the most serious he had since he had bidden the policemen enter the house, and McMurrough merely sat in thoughtful mood, gently rubbing his bruises, as his partner ushered Falconer and Carmichael out of the house.

Back beside their cars, Carmichael was also looking introspective, and when Falconer asked him what he was thinking about, he replied, 'I'm just glad I'm not famous, that's all.'

Chapter Two

Tuesday
Fairmile Green

At Glass House, there was a ring on the doorbell at eight-thirty the next morning, catching both inhabitants still in bed, and necessitating Radcliffe to run downstairs in his dressing gown and slippers, for McMurrough would no more have volunteered to go down to answer it himself than fly to the moon.

On the doorstep, stood two men in smart bottle-green uniforms, one man positioned slightly behind the other. Radcliffe had no idea that he was witnessing a well-rehearsed delivery pattern, and just stood there, dumbfounded, wondering what on earth this was all about.

'Good morning, sir,' intoned the man in front. 'PPP at your service this lovely morning, sir' As he said this, he thrust a large cardboard box into Radcliffe's arms, while his partner moved to the front, announcing, 'And here is the little precious himself: one miniature dachshund, for your enjoyment – registered name "Dipsy Daxie". If you'll just sign this receipt, sir, we wish you many happy years with your new pet.'

'What the hell's going on?' asked Radcliffe, as he hurriedly put the box on the ground to accept the wire cage that was thrust at him, a tiny form curled up inside it. And what the heck's PPP?' He'd signed the receipt and taken charge of the cage before he could gather his wits sufficiently to realise what he'd just done.

'Posh Pet Procurement, Mr McMurrough. Thank you for using our service,' replied the first man in explanation, then they both turned on their heels and walked off the property, got into their van, and drove off, leaving Radcliffe standing on the doorstep with a look on his face that declared that he had just been royally done over.

'CHADWICK!' he yelled, loud enough to waken the dead, or at least a very lazy partner. 'What the hell's this elongated rat you seem to have purchased for? Dinner?' and was not impressed when Chadwick came bounding down the stairs with the proud look of young motherhood on his face, making little kissing noises and crooning, 'Dipsy, darling, come to Daddy, and just ignore cross old Auntie Bailey.'

Auntie Bailey's face would have looked more at home in the Old Bailey, as a witness for the prosecution, especially when 'Dipsy darling' woke up and began to howl miserably at the absence of his mother and siblings.

'And if you think you're going to fob off walking that thing on me, you can think again. I will *not* – I repeat – I will *not* be seen in public exercising a saveloy on a lead. That thing looks like a cocktail sausage on four sticks.

'As far as I'm concerned, Dappy Dixie, or whatever the thing's called, is all yours. You're the one who's going to be feeding it, walking it, and bathing it. Me, I'm nothing to do with it. This is your toy, kid, and you can leave me right out of it. I've suddenly developed a severe allergy to dogs.'

'That's Dipsy Daxie, if you don't mind. Kindly remember his name, as he is now one of the family.' Chadwick had taken the little animal out of its cage and was cuddling it like a baby. 'Just you ignore nasty old Auntie Bailey; it must be the time of the month, he's such an old grump-pot.'

'And you can sort out the contents of that bloody great box as well. I'm not having that in the hall for a fortnight while you get round to it.' Bailey was working up quite a head of steam, in his indignation that his partner could have ordered such a thing – and after the peacocks, too – without a word of consultation, too – that he felt he could easily burst.

Characteristically, Chadwick ignored his partner's protests and sat down on the floor to unpack his goodie-box. 'Lead and collar; check. Feeding bowl and water bowl; check. Squeaky toys; check. Soft toys; check. Pooper scooper; check. Wicker basket and blanket for sleeping; check ...'

'You haven't listened to a word I've said, have you, you little git,' Bailey protested crossly.

'Nope.'

At this cold-hearted and negative response, Bailey 'took his bum in his hands', threw open the multi-fold glass doors to the back garden, and went out in a huff, Chadwick's voice floating after him.

'And when you get back indoors, there's been enough talk about other things. I suggest we get back to me, and talk about something really interesting.'

Bailey was back within two minutes, nursing a bloodied hand.

'What've you done, cut yourself on that sharp tongue of yours?' queried McMurrough, sarcastically. And shut the doors. 'My little treasure may get out before he's ready.'

'Damn your little treasure! One of your blasted peacocks has bitten me.'

'I believe you'll find that's "pecked". They don't have teeth.'

'And neither will you, if you don't start being just a little more civil,' his bloodied but unbowed partner snapped and, with that, Bailey took himself upstairs to the first-aid kit, whereupon he found that Chadwick had opened to their fullest extent, the matching multi-fold doors in the master-suite at the rear of the house, and a fine collection of flying insects had taken advantage of the opportunity to come in and have a free viewing.

Wednesday
Market Darley

Falconer had thoroughly enjoyed the first of Carmichael's full days back in the office and would have appreciated it even more, had he known it would be his last peaceful day for quite a while. And this evening he was having dinner with Heather. Life was grand at the moment, and he didn't even consider this newly established even tenor not continuing. He dressed with care as a mark of respect for his companion, then picked her up from the nurses' home where she was staying while her flat in the Midlands was waiting to be sold.

They had a regular booking at a little Italian restaurant in the Market Square, flexible enough to allow for their respective jobs and the vagaries of the hours of these diverse but, in many ways, similar careers. Heather had nursed the owner's wife through a gallstone operation about six months ago, and he was still grateful for the way she had sat with her and coaxed her to eat, when she felt she'd never be able to face food again.

Their table was booked for seven-thirty, reasonably early, but it gave them half a chance of getting at least one course down their throats, before one of them was summoned on an unplanned call-out, and they had plenty to talk about tonight. Heather had been involved in dealing with the victims of a multi-car pile-up on the road south into Market Darley; the consequence, it seemed, of urban-dwelling tourists and their lack of experience on such narrow country roads, although to the locals, that particular road was judged to be a good-sized one. It happened at least once every summer, and when the first of last year's had occurred she had just started working at the hospital.

At the end of her tale, Falconer asked her if she knew when he had first noticed her at the hospital and, when she replied that she didn't, proceeded to describe the scene that had so caught his eye.

'You were standing at the bed next to Carmichael's, holding one of those pressed cardboard bowls, when the patient in the bed suddenly projectile vomited all down your front. Instead of being angry or disgusted, you just started laughing uproariously at your plight, eventually getting the patient to join in, at the state of your uniform.

'That was probably the best medicine you could have offered him; no apologies and embarrassment, just a damned good laugh. Then, when you leaned over to tear off some of that all-purpose hospital paper, I noticed a little ladder in the left leg of your tights just lengthen another half inch. I couldn't take my eyes off that tiny imperfection growing totally without your knowledge, and I realised I wanted to talk to you.'

'I remember the incident well, and we did seem to meet in the canteen quite frequently after that,' she replied.

'And by Carmichael's bedside,' he added.

'Which was *my* doing,' she chimed in. 'I rather wanted to get to know you too, as your visits seemed to do Davey so much good. I say, this carbonara's absolutely ace, isn't it?'

'I'll say. Are you going to have zabaglione for dessert? And I'll tell you what I've been up to.'

Having hailed the waiter and ordered their final course, he told her about Carmichael coming back to the office on Monday night, yesterday being his first full day back in harness. 'You make sure you don't work poor Davey too hard. He's had a very bad time of it, as you well know, over the last couple of months.'

'"Poor Davey", as you insist on calling that great big lump, was thrilled to bits with the call-out we had Monday night.'

'You didn't get him out late, did you, you cruel beast? I told you, the boy needs his rest. You really are a slave driver.'

'He'd never have forgiven me if I hadn't taken him with me. The call was only to Chadwick McMurrough's house.'

'No!' she squeaked, not even giving him time to ask her if she'd ever heard of him. 'Not that brightly dressed camp guy with the chat show?'

'That's the one,' agreed Falconer.

'Ooh! I think he's lovely. I was rooting for him all the way through *The Glass House* and I watched him in *Cockneys*.' Here she paused as if in amusing memory. 'And I never miss one of his chat shows. If I'm on duty I have to record it; he's just so funny. I wish I could have gone with you; I'd love to meet him, although I'd probably die of embarrassment.'

'So, you're a closet Chadwick fan, are you?' asked Falconer, in surprise. This was exactly the sort of thing that happened when you only met up once a fortnight.

'Not exactly "closet", and I had no idea he'd moved into the area. Where did you say he was?'

'Fairmile Green.'

Fairmile Green

'I'm going to take Dipsy for a little walk,' announced Chadwick. 'You coming, Bailey?'

'Are you out of your tiny little mind?' his partner responded. 'When I said I wouldn't be seen dead with that mobile chorizo, I meant it. I'm going to have a little nap, then, when you get back, I might deign to accompany you to the local hostelry for a little liquid refreshment.

'If you're lucky, there might be some fans of yours there, and you can sit and bask in their admiration, before we come back here and retire for the night. That sort of thing always puts you in a good mood.'

'Suit yourself, sweetie, but I'm off.'

'I hope none of the neighbours dies laughing.'

'Bitch!'

'Silly cow! Have a nice walk with your mini-Cumberland.'

Radcliffe stretched himself out on the extra-long, white leather sofa and was asleep within minutes, his snoring, for once, unappreciated by either man or beast.

The next thing of which he was aware was the echo of what he immediately identified as a howl of pain, followed by some very rich and loud swearing, and a face appeared at the rear glass doors, filled with anguish.

Leaping to his feet and making a rush for the doors, he unlatched them and admitted Chadwick, clutching one shoulder with one hand, the other, limply clutching the lead of the tiny pup.

As Radcliffe grabbed the lead and pulled the dog inside, Chadwick began to groan with pain, and to insist that Bailey called the police once more and, if necessary, a doctor.

'What in the name of God has happened?'

'I decided to come in the back way so that Dipsy could do any business he needed to conduct in the garden before we came in, and maybe he'd not need to go while we're out. But when I opened the side gate, a bloody great stone, which must have been balanced on the top, fell off and landed on my shoulder. I'm sure it's broken.'

'Your shoulder would never break a stone. Where did you leave it? By the gate?'

'You unfeeling bitch!'

'Come here and let me see.'

'I'm in agony here, and all you can do is insult me,' replied McMurrough, stripping off his long-sleeved T-shirt to reveal a slight graze and a swelling that would turn, overnight, into quite a satisfactory bruise.

223

'You big baby! There's no way that's broken, but it looks pretty painful.'

'What if it had landed on my head?'

'Then the thickness of your skull definitely would have shattered it.'

'Cow! What if it had landed on Dipsy? It would have killed him.'

'That's true. I think you're right about reporting this. After that episode the other evening, we'd better just give the police a ring. Better safe than paying for a funeral.' Radcliffe was all heart. 'But you don't need to waste a doctor's time. All he'd do would be to send you for an x-ray. Do you really want to spend the evening hanging around in A&E?'

'No way, but you could ring me mum as well. I could do with a bit of TLC, and I'm not likely to get that from you in a million years,' requested McMurrough.

'Sod your mum. What's that stunted frankfurter doing on the new wooden floor. Hey, stop that this minute! And what are you looking so glum about?'

'It'll be too late to go to the pub if we have to wait for the police.'

'Tough, you spoiled little brat.'

Market Darley
While Heather was still cross-questioning Falconer about Chadwick McMurrough's new residence, his mobile phone rang, putting paid to the flow of questions for a few minutes. When he ended the call, he smiled at her and said, 'I've got to go over to Fairmile Green again. There's been another attack, albeit a minor one, on our nine days' wonder local celebrity. Would you care to accompany me?'

'You bet your life I would. Just hang on while I get the rest of this zabaglione down my neck, and we can get straight off,' replied, Heather, beginning to spoon her dessert into her mouth with almost unbelievable speed. 'There, finished. Let's go!' she announced, only to be stalled by her dinner partner, who chose to finish his at his leisure, calling for the bill and not rushing himself. Falconer was cool, or so he secretly believed.

'Take off your shoes,' ordered Heather, in a rather brusque manner, and quite inexplicably.

'Why on earth do you want me to do that?'

'So I can count your toes. At the moment I'd put money on you only having three – you sloth.'

Fairmile Green

Falconer hadn't bothered disturbing Carmichael over this call, and had informed Bob Bryant that he would go alone – at least technically alone – and Bob agreed with this decision. It didn't sound very serious, and the sergeant would need a bit more rest than usual, having just returned to work; and Falconer didn't even want to think about having to summon DC Roberts, not when his evening, thus far, had been delightful.

Radcliffe must have been watching out for the car from the dining room window, for the door was opened before the two of them had even got through the gate. 'Is it OK if my friend comes in?' asked Falconer, as they approached the front door, 'Only we were having supper when I received the call that you'd had another spot of bother.'

'No problem,' Bailey replied. 'We've already got Chadwick's ever-loving mother here: the more the merrier.' The man did not seem best pleased at the way the house was filling up. With these two, that would now make five adults, a ridiculously shaped puppy, and God knew how many fancy birds at the back.

In the lounge they found McMurrough, sitting mournfully on the over-sized sofa, his arm in a sling, his face like a wet weekend. 'Good evening, Mr

McMurrough,' Falconer greeted him. 'I hope you don't mind, but I was in a restaurant having a meal with my friend when I got the call to come here, and it seemed churlish, if not time-wasting, not to come straight here.'

'Be my guest,' the invalid replied. 'You can see for yourselves what agony I'm in,' and he winced theatrically and put a hand to his injured shoulder. There didn't seem to be anyone else in the room, until a voice uttered from behind a large white leather armchair, its back to them, and facing a very large television set which burbled away quietly.

Above the sound of the television, the voice suddenly opined, 'Great big girl's blouse. Talk about making a mountain out of a molehill. But then you always were a jessie.'

At their expressions of surprise, McMurrough said, 'You haven't met my mother, have you? She's the one in front of the TV with a tray of blinis, cream cheese, smoked salmon, and caviar on her lap. Say "hello", Mummy Dearest.'

Falconer and Heather took a few paces down the room and saw the middle-aged woman, sitting in the chair like a malignant goddess guarding her ambrosial snack. 'I made 'im three slices of toast, cheese, and tomato and a huge mug of 'ot chocolate,' the deity proclaimed, 'and that's all the TLC 'e's getting from me for one night. From the phone call, I thought 'e must be dying, at the very least, and there 'e is, with just a knocked shoulder.

'Can you keep this mobile canine thing orf me slippers, somebody? I don't want to 'ave to give it a kick.'

'Would you like to get back home now, Mummy McMurrough?' asked Bailey, and she nodded.

'I'll just get me shoes on and collect me 'andbag, and I'll be orf.' To Falconer, she added, 'Always wanted to be rich and famous when 'e were a kiddy, 'e did. Well, 'e's got it now, much good it's doing 'im. I've always said that you should be careful what you ask for, because you just might get it.'

'Does Mr McMurrough have any brothers or sisters?' asked the inspector, wondering if there could be any sibling rivalry behind these two recent mishaps.

''E's got three, but they're blood strangers now. They don't approve of 'im making a public spectacle of 'isself.'

'If you don't mind me saying so, Mrs McMurrough, you don't sound as if you come from the same place as your son; your accents are so dissimilar.'

'I should 'ope so, too. 'E were always tryin' to talk posh, from when 'e were a kid. Traitor to 'is roots, 'e is, but do you 'ear me complainin'? No, you don't. I've always told 'im to be 'oo 'e feels 'e is, and tell the rest of the world to go 'ang, and that's exac'ly what 'e's done. Can't say fairer than that, can yer?'

'Your attitude says much for your magnanimity,' replied Falconer, just before a plaintive voice spoke from the sofa.

'I *am* in the room, you know. And I *don't* appreciate being talked about in front of me like that.' McMurrough was missing the limelight. 'If you wish to dissect my character, kindly do it behind my back.'

And it was definitely going to be much too late to go to the pub tonight.

As Radcliffe ushered Mummy McMurrough out to the car, Falconer introduced Heather, and let her have a little gush in front of him, before he began his questioning.

When the two of them left half an hour later, Falconer promising to get someone out to collect the 'weapon', and any forensic evidence there may be, he said to Heather, 'Shall we go back to mine for a coffee? It's still quite early.'

'Great idea,' she replied. 'And there's something I need to ask you.' Leaving that threat hanging like a sword of Damocles, she enquired whether he'd like her to come over and cook Sunday roast for him, if both of them were off duty. It was quite a forward suggestion from her, as the invitation for coffee had overstepped bounds already set, and it would be her first visit to his home.

Having agreed in a somewhat nervous state, to this unexpected and unprecedented offer, the inspector spent the rest of the short drive back to Market Darley telling her about the traditional Sunday meal during his childhood years.

He had noticed, through the window of Glass House, a large floral centrepiece in the middle of the dining table. There had been no centrepiece in his home. Cook had always brought the lump of charred flesh to the table, and set it before his father with a defiant glare, which was returned in silent venom.

Every Sunday morning, his father would remind Cook that all of them like their meat pink, with the exception of chicken. Every Sunday lunchtime, he waged war on the tough, stringy lumps of charred meat, with which his ever-hopeful carving knife was presented.

The exception was, of course, the rare treat (in those days) of a chicken, which oozed dark pink juices as soon as he pierced its skin. Falconer Senior felt true hatred for the cook, who remained his *bête noir*, until he finally sacked her after a memorable Sunday when he had become incandescent with rage at the dry, solid, dark lump that sat, seemingly mocking him, from the carving plate.

He finally lost his grip on his temper, and wrestled the blasted lump off the plate, across the table and, eventually, to the floor, at which point Mrs Falconer had rung for Cook, requested that she open a tin of corned beef, then pack her bags forthwith, and leave the premises on a permanent basis.

Thereafter, the carving was always carried out in the kitchen, with silent savagery and frustration, by the matriarch of the family.

Heather laughed gleefully at the visions of this in her mind's eye, and declared that Sundays were never so dramatic in her childhood home, and suggested that this was probably because they couldn't afford to pay the wages of a cook.

While Falconer escorted his lady friend into his house, Chadwick McMurrough and Bailey Radcliffe in Fairmile Green settled down to watch McMurrough's chat show that they had recorded to watch at their leisure, Dipsy Daxie curled up, fast asleep, on his new master's lap, while Bailey leaned across and played lazily with the puppy's ears.

Back in Market Darley, the sense of tension began to grow in Falconer as Heather entered his home, and their coffee together became quite a stiff affair. He had few visitors, and the entrance of someone with whom he met regularly for social reasons bothered him more greatly than he had anticipated.

When he went to bed that night, it was with a real sense of foreboding and doom.

The Falconer Files

by

Andrea Frazer

For more information about **Andrea Frazer**
and other **Accent Press** titles
please visit

www.accentpress.co.uk